Can You Feel
the Thunder?

Can You Feel the Thunder?

LYNN E. MCELFRESH

Atheneum Books for Young Readers

Atheneum Books for Young Readers
An imprint of Simon & Schuster Children's Publishing Division
1230 Avenue of the Americas
New York, New York 10020

Book design by Nina Barnett
The text of this book is set in New Baskerville

Printed in the United States of America
10 9 8 7 6

Library of Congress Cataloging-in-Publication Data
McElfresh, Lynn E.
Can you feel the thunder? / Lynn E. McElfresh.—1st ed.
p.   cm.
Summary: Thirteen-year-old Mic Parsons struggles with mixed feelings about
his deaf and blind sister while at the same time he makes his way through the tur-
moils of junior high.
ISBN 0-689-82324-X
[1. Brothers and sisters—Fiction. 2. Blind—Fiction. 3. Deaf—Fiction. 4.
Physically handicapped—Fiction.] I. Title.
PZ7.M4784475Can   1999
[Fic]—dc21   98-36609

To Carol Dapogny and all middle school
English teachers who ignite a passion for writing
in their students

Special thanks to Mrs. Buttz's seventh grade
enriched English class for their candid feedback

Chapter 1

If you're looking for *WEIRD*, you can find it on Bixby Court. Old Man Petrowski, who lives at 422, has webbed fingers. Across the street from him is 425—the only Pepto-Bismol pink house in our town, probably the whole universe. Next door to the Pepto house lives Sam, the three-legged golden retriever. And then there is Mrs. Marston at 418. She claims she saw the ghost of Houdini when she was eleven and was on *Oprah* last year to tell the world about it.

And I, Mic Parsons, live at 412 Bixby Court with a freaky fifteen-year-old sister and a bratty four-year-old brother. Believe me, our family is strange even for Bixby Court, but it looks like new competition just moved in.

"There's the new boy," Dad said as we backed down the driveway.

The new kid tossed back his stringy black hair and stood up on the pedals of his bike. He was wearing a light-colored jacket over light-colored jeans. Even from down the block, I could see huge glasses on a big nose. Instead of a book bag, he had a newspaper carrier's bag slung over his shoulder.

"He's about your age," Dad said. As Dad slowed down, the kid pedaled faster. He pushed his glasses up on his nose as he passed us. He never looked in our direction.

Snubbed by a nerd.

"Chortle . . ."

"What?"

"I think their last name is Chortle."

Weirder than weird, I thought.

Weirdness is attracted to Bixby Court. So why was I surprised that the new kid turns out to be the poster child for Nerds of America?

"Make sure you introduce yourself to him," Dad said. "Starting junior high in March is tough."

Me? Friends with that nerd? As if my life wasn't already weird enough. I'm stuck with my family, but *I* decide who my friends are. No way would I even think about talking to this kid.

"Vern Chortle."

I looked up from my pizza.

Oh, my God. It was the nerd! He was sitting down across from me at our lunch table. The newspaper carrier bag dropped to the floor with a thud. He must have every schoolbook he owned in it. He slid the lunch tray to the table, plopped on the bench where Stolks usually sat, and started shoveling in mystery meat.

No one sits at this table during B lunch period but Stolks, Freemont, and me. It's our table. Wildman Freemont is my best friend. We've been in the same class since second grade. Until this year, that is. This year, we only have consumer ed and lunch together. Our lunch table is sacred.

As soon as he sat down, Nerd Boy took a laminated layout of the school out of his bag. He peeled a neon orange sticker from the corner and put it in the square marked lunchroom. I couldn't resist peeking at it. It read YOU ARE HERE.

"I saw you this morning," Nerd Boy said through a mouthful of cooked carrots and peas. "Your dad was driving you to school. You live down the street from me."

I was too shocked to answer.

"Who's this?" Freemont asked, tossing a hoagie on the table before he folded up his long legs and sat down.

"Chortle," I replied.

"What?" Freemont asked.

Stolks froze when he saw the geek in his seat. He walked around to our side of the table and sat down clutching his mammoth lunch bag in front of him. I felt the bench groan under his weight.

The three of us sat on one side of the table staring at Nerd Boy.

Nerd Boy ate nonstop. He looked at each of us as he shoveled in mashed potatoes.

None of us was eating. Even Stolks sat with his mouth open but his bag unopened, staring at the new kid.

"Who is this?" Freemont asked again.

"Vern Chortle," Nerd Boy said, pushing a drip of gravy back into his mouth.

"Vern?" Freemont asked.

"Chortle," I repeated. What was his mother thinking of? Wasn't Chortle bad enough? Did she have to make it worse and name the kid Vernon on top of it? He didn't just have *nerd* written all over him; it was written in permanent marker.

"Where did *it* come from?" Freemont asked.

"Moved here from Cincinnati last weekend. I live down the street from Four-Twelve," he said, pointing to me with a brick-hard roll. He crunched into it.

"Four-Twelve?"

"Four twelve Bixby Court," he said. He wrestled another bite from the roll. "I think we have a couple of classes together, Four-Twelve," he said, as tiny bits of hard roll spewed out of his mouth.

His watch started beeping. He jumped to his feet and pressed a button to make it stop. "Wish I could stay and talk, but I have to meet Ms. Sturgel, my counselor. New-kid-in-school stuff. We'll talk later."

He stood and lifted the strap over his head and balanced the heavy load of books on his hip. He grabbed his tray and walked away. At the garbage can, he turned and waved. No smile. Just a wave.

It was then I noticed his socks. They were fire-engine red.

We watched him leave the lunchroom. I hadn't eaten a bite of my pizza since he had sat down. Cold school pizza is deadly. Once the cheese cools, it hardens and you begin to wonder what it's really made of.

"Professional nerd," Freemont decided.

Stolks ripped into his lunch. "Yeah," he agreed as he attacked his sandwich.

"I don't know," I said. "He didn't have a pocket protector."

Chapter 2

The next day, Nerd Boy was wearing all light colors again. It must be the Nerd's official uniform. A pale-colored short-sleeved shirt with a button-down collar over light-colored jeans.

He sat across from us again, moved the YOU ARE HERE sticker on his school layout, shoveled in food with lightning speed, and spoke to us between bites about special placement tests he had to take after school. "So, I won't be able to walk home with you tonight, Four-Twelve. Maybe tomorrow."

His watch alarm beeped and he jumped up to empty his tray.

Today his socks were a bright neon green. Did I see lights blinking from his ankles?

"They're electric," he said to me from the garbage can just loud enough for me to hear but not loud enough to attract attention in the noisy lunchroom.

He raised his foot and lifted his pant leg slightly so I could see the multicolored lights that flashed as they ran up his leg.

"Socks. They're my thing. Three hundred and eighty-two pairs. You'll have to come by and see them sometime. See ya, Four-Twelve." He waved again. No smile. He hadn't cracked a smile in the two days I'd known him.

"Four-Twelve?" Freemont asked.

"Four twelve Bixby Court. My address," I reminded Freemont. "I feel like a spy. Agent Four-Twelve reporting!" I saluted Freemont.

"I have to change my classification of him from Nerd to Weirdo. No! Mental Case." Freemont snorted through his big nose. "If that Mental Case sits here tomorrow, I'll throw him out."

Stolks grunted in approval as he shoved a Twinkie into his face.

"Careful, Freemont. He could have nuclear attack socks," I said.

Stolks laughed.

"He really has attached himself to you. Is there something you aren't telling us?" Freemont asked, raising just one eyebrow at me.

"Yeah, right." I rolled my eyes.

"I mean compared to what goes on in your house, this guy probably is real normal."

Stolks laughed as he sucked down another Twinkie.

I rolled my eyes again. Inside, my stomach clutched the pizza and rolled over.

Nerd Boy was right. We had two afternoon classes together, social studies and gym. I have no idea how he knew that. How could he have guessed? He didn't even know my name. He only knew my street number. Four-Twelve. Maybe he's an alien.

In both classes, he waved (no smile) and said, "Hi, Four-Twelve." I moved my hand with only a mere hint of a wave and tried to ignore him.

I've never met anyone so geeky looking. He's probably a computer nerd, a mathematical, scientific genius . . . but totally out of it. Why had he attached himself to me? I had enough weirdness in my life! Living at 412 Bixby Court with my weird family was bad enough. No way would I let some nerd ruin school for me.

I hoped the placement tests put him in some special program for kids with electric socks.

Chapter 3

There are two things I hate about Jefferson Junior High School: math and locker 764. Mom keeps telling me I make my own fate. Bull! I tried to change both math *and* my locker but Ms. Sturgel, my counselor, said I would just have to make the best of the situation.

I've never liked math, especially fractions. But fractions junior high style with Ms. Rothchild are even worse. Math before fractions wasn't that bad. I teetered between a B and a C first semester. Now, I don't know if I'll pass. Fractions stink.

Mom is convinced I'd get an A if I just *applied myself.* She's never met Ms. Rothchild. At least, not the *real* Ms. Rothchild. She really *is* out to get me. I bet she sits up nights thinking of ways to torture me. Mom says I'm paranoid.

Ms. Rothchild's hate for me plus fractions equals an F— which is exactly what I received on my math quiz today.

"I don't want your parents to just *sign* your quiz. On the back, I want them to write how they *feel* about your grade," she said to all us poor slobs who received a D or an F on the quiz. Tell me she didn't sit up half the night thinking up that one! I'd be grounded for the whole weekend for sure.

"I'll tell her how I feel about it," I murmured as I opened locker 764.

Two seconds later, I heard elephant footsteps approaching. "Get your locker door out of my way," it bellowed.

She must have radar. Even if I only spent three seconds a day at my locker, Godzilla Girl would be there at those precise seconds complaining that *I* was in *her* way. If she wasn't so huge, we'd all have more room. If I had my way, I would be in an all-guy hall—just Stolks, Freemont, Davidson, Willowby, and me.

"Here, Mic, I'll give you more room." Someone tapped me on my shoulder.

Oh, God. When did *she* walk up?

What rotten luck. *Parsons* fit alphabetically between the two most undesirable girls at Jefferson Junior High—pesty Julia Patterson and Penny (Godzilla Girl) Parrish. I can't stand either of them. I wish I could change my name to Mic *Zwoyer* and get away from everyone!

"I couldn't help seeing the math test you put in your folder," Julia said.

"It would help if you didn't look over my shoulder," I said.

She giggled.

"I'm good at fractions. If you'd like to study together, just give me a call." She was beet red now.

"Do you mind?" Godzilla Girl growled. She kicked my backpack in my direction so hard, my locker door shut on my hand.

"Don't forget," Julia said. "You. Me. Math. Anytime." She put a purple piece of notebook paper on top of my books.

Gag me.

"Coming, Mic? Or can't you tear yourself away from your girlfriends?" Freemont called.

"Right." I grabbed my jacket from the hook, slammed my locker, and clicked the lock in place.

"Bye, Mic!" Julia giggled.

"Bye, Julia," Freemont answered in a singsongy voice. "Mic will give you a big good-bye kiss later."

I elbowed him in the stomach.

"What's this?" Freemont asked, pulling the folded purple notebook paper off my stack of books.

"Give it back." I had no idea what flaky Julia Patterson had written. I did know I didn't want Freemont to read it.

"Ooooh. Purple."

"Give it back." I lunged for the paper.

"And purple ink, too." He sniffed at the paper and jerked it out of my reach and handed it to Stolks, who had walked up behind me. "What do you think, Stolksie? Does it smell like Midnight Passion or Kiss Me Quick?"

Stolks sniffed the paper and shrugged. Just as I was about to jerk the paper from Stolks's hands, Freemont reached over the top of me and grabbed it back.

"Give it back, Freemont."

"Well, if it really means that much to you . . ."

"No! Keep it! I don't care," I said. I crashed through the door and out into the March wind.

"Julia Patterson," Freemont read from the note. "555-9347. Call anytime."

"I'm not listening," I called back to Freemont.

"She dotted her *i*'s with little hearts," he called after me.

Chapter 4

It's March. That dead month between basketball and baseball season. Dreary. Nothing to do after school but go home.

Basketball practice had been every afternoon. Freemont was never much of a basketball player. He didn't go out for the team this year. But on weekends Freemont, Stolks, and I went down to the rec hall and played two on one. Even with all that practice, I had played a grand total of seven minutes and thirty-nine seconds of basketball during the season. Four minutes of that came in the game against Roosevelt when two of our first-stringers fouled out and a third twisted his ankle in the last quarter of the game.

Even though I didn't get to play much, basketball had kept me in shape for baseball. It also had kept me out of the house. Now, I had nothing to keep me from going home with Ms. Rothchild's test for Mom to sign.

I knew the verdict before it ever left Mom's mouth.

Grounded.

She didn't want to hear how Ms. Rothchild was out to get me. She wouldn't listen when I told her I just couldn't get fractions.

"And don't think you are going to spend all weekend lying around watching TV and playing Nintendo," she added.

I rolled my eyes. It was going to be a long weekend.

"Do you have any idea of how you are going to spend your time?"

"Rearranging my baseball card collection?" I knew better than to say it. But I did anyway.

She just glared at me.

"I studied for this test. I don't get fractions. I could spend all weekend studying. I just don't understand them."

"Attitude. What the mind can conceive and believe, it can achieve."

As if on cue, Stephanie shuffled into the room.

"Look at your sister. I've never heard the words *I can't* come out of her mouth."

And if they did, you wouldn't understand what she said, I thought.

"If anyone has reasons to make excuses . . ." She stopped and swallowed hard. "Apply yourself. It's all in your attitude."

There, she did it. She managed to squeeze her two favorite *A* words into one breath. *Apply* and *attitude.*

Leave it to Ms. Rothchild to return a bad test on a Thursday. If she had waited just one more day, I could have put off showing the test to Mom until Sunday night or Monday morning. Now my whole weekend was ruined. I should have taken my chances with detention.

The doorbell rang and I opened the door to see Nerd Boy standing on the doorstep. He was out of uniform. He was wearing a pair of sweatpants and a New York Mets T-shirt. He was holding a large plastic cup out in front of him.

I wondered if he was collecting for Nerds of America.

"Mic's grounded," Mom said from behind me.

"Oh, I'm not here to see Four-Twelve. Sugar."

"Excuse me?"

"Sugar. I'm Vern Chortle. We moved into four twenty-eight at the end of the cul-de-sac. From Cincinnati. I came to borrow a cup of sugar."

Mom's cheeks reddened.

I couldn't resist looking down at his socks. They were bright red. Not the same red socks he had on the first day. These had holly leaves and big green letters that said HO-HO-HO.

"I'm sorry. I thought you and Mic were friends. You're about the same age," Mom stammered.

"We're NOT," I said.

"The same age?" Mom asked.

"I'm thirteen," Nerd Boy volunteered.

"Friends," I finished.

Nerd Boy was still holding the plastic measuring cup out in front of him.

"Where are my manners? Please come in. What grade are you in?" she asked.

Why do parents ask such stupid questions? If he was thirteen, of course he would be in the seventh grade at Jefferson Junior High School. So why did she act surprised when he told her we were in the same grade?

"Do you have any classes together?" she asked, pulling the sugar canister forward.

"Four-Twelve and I have fifth and sixth hour together— social studies and gym."

Mom had just started scooping sugar out of the canister when I heard Stephanie clomping down the hall again. I cringed. I don't know when I started to be embarrassed by Stephanie, but I hadn't had anyone over for a while.

"Did you just need one cup or two?" Mom asked.

Stephanie stepped into the kitchen. It looked like she had tried to comb her hair again. It frizzed out wildly from her head and had a big clump in the side with a barrette sticking out of it. She had a huge smile on her face.

Stephanie started to make her way across the kitchen. She had a half-full glass of lemonade in her hand and was shuffling on a collision course with Nerd Boy. Mom was busy interrogating Nerd Boy and measuring out sugar. She didn't seem to notice Stephanie at all. Nerd Boy turned away from Stephanie like he hadn't noticed anything different or strange about her.

I was panicked. My heart pounded in my chest. I jumped between Stephanie and Nerd Boy at the last possible moment. Stephanie ran right into me. Lemonade sloshed down the front of both of us. She should have been mad, but she still had that stupid grin on her face. Her eyes rolled back into her head and she let out a "MY-Y-Y-Y-Y-Y!" in her shrill nasal voice. That's her word for me, *My-y-y-y*. She can't say *Michael* or even *Mic*. *K*'s are too hard for her to pronounce.

Stephanie reached back and put the lemonade on the table and dabbed at the wet spot on her front.

I'm not sure, but I think Nerd Boy got a bit of lemonade shower, too. If he did, he didn't say anything about it.

"Oh, this is Mic's sister, Stephanie," Mom said like she just noticed Stephanie in the room.

Stephanie clomped right past Nerd Boy on her way to the sink, where she was pulling a few too many paper towels off the roll. She was going to clean up the mess on the floor.

Quickly, I leaped to her side, took the paper towels from her hands, and wiped up the mess.

Stephanie signed "thank you." "Tank ooouuuu, My-y-y-y-y," she wailed. Her voice was always too loud, very nasal and monotone. It seemed even louder to me when other people were around. She still had a big grin on her face.

Mom reached over and fingerspelled in her hand that we had a visitor.

Stephanie's eyes brightened. She put her arm out to see if she could feel who our guest was.

I watched Nerd Boy for a reaction. He acted like he saw people like Stephanie every day.

"Well, Vern, let me walk you to the door," I said, grabbing him by the arm. I pulled him into the living room before he could say or do *anything*. If I hurried, I could get him out the door before . . .

"Wait a minute," Mom said. "Stephanie would like to meet our new neighbor."

"Mom!" I cried. I hated when Mom did this. But it was too late. She led Stephanie into the living room.

"This is V-E-R-N C-H-O-R-T-L-E." Mom fingerspelled the letters into her hand. "Our new neighbor."

Stephanie laughed at the name. She reached out and felt Nerd Boy's stringy hair. She felt the big glasses and her hand ended up on his huge nose. She didn't hide the laugh that escaped from her constant smile. It was as if she could feel how funny he looked.

"Do you have any brothers or sisters?" Mom asked Nerd Boy.

"Two sisters," Nerd Boy replied. "One older, one younger."

Stephanie must have thought he was talking to her. She put her hand on his neck and reached for his hand to see if he was fingerspelling.

"Almost like Mic." Mom nodded. "Stephanie is his older sister and he has a younger brother."

"Where from?" I saw Stephanie sign to Mom.

"C-I-N-C-I-N-N-A-T-I," Mom fingerspelled back.

A momentary look of confusion crossed Stephanie's face. "State?" she asked.

I took the opportunity to get Nerd Boy to the door.

"I'm sure your mom is waiting for you *and* the sugar. Don't let us keep you."

"Thanks," he said without a smile. "Later, Four-Twelve." And he was gone.

Chapter 5

Before Nerd Boy reached his house with the cup of sugar, Mom had the relief map of the United States on the kitchen table. She showed Stephanie where Ohio was on the map, then she led her fingers to where we lived in Illinois. Stephanie traced the path from Ohio to Illinois over and over as if her fingers would tell her how many miles separated the two states.

United States geography and history are two of Stephanie's favorite subjects.

"C-A-P-I-T-A-L C-O-L-U-M-B-U-S," she spelled to me.

Stephanie knows all the state capitals and the names of the U.S. presidents. She can fingerspell them in order at lightning speed.

"O-H-I-O, birth state for seven U.S. presidents," she signed. "Know who?" she signed to me.

Her big, blank blue eyes flitted back in her head. She smiled her big smile, tilted her head to one side, and waited for me to answer. The light from the window bounced off her frizzy hair, making it seem almost alive.

"G-R-A-N-T, H-A-Y-E-S, G-A-R . . ." she began signing.

I went to my room, shut the door, and plopped on my bed. As soon as I hit the bed, I remembered the lemonade. Uck! Sticky! I pulled my shirt over my head and tossed it on the heap on my closet floor.

I hated when Mom introduced Stephanie and never explained what was wrong with her. Mom works with deaf and blind people every day so I guess she figures everyone knows about them.

I pulled a clean shirt from my dresser. Before I could pull it over my head, Stephanie clomped down the hall and tried to push my bedroom door open. I stood in front of it.

The door popped open and I slammed against it with all my weight, shutting it again. Stephanie's much smaller than I am although she's two years older. She looks more like a nine-year-old than a fifteen-year-old. Still, she's strong.

She bumped the door open again and I pushed it shut. I braced myself up against the door. *"Mom,"* I yelled.

Stephanie's throaty "MY-Y-Y-Y-Y-Y-Y" was all I could hear on the other side of the door.

I threw my head back and shut my eyes. *"Mom,"* I yelled again.

Mom showed up and eased the door open. "What's going on here?"

"Stephanie won't leave me alone," I told her. "I'm trying to change clothes."

"It's not like she can *see* anything, Mic," Mom said, like I was retarded.

"Can't a guy have *any* privacy in this house?"

"Stephanie just wants to talk to you about your new friend," Mom said.

"He's *not* my new friend and I *don't* want to talk."

Mom looked at me funny and pulled Stephanie into the hall.

"What for?" I heard Stephanie ask in her nasal monotone voice.

Mom's reply was silent. I knew she was signing and only mouthing the words.

Stephanie ended up in her room across the hall. I heard something hit the floor.

Stephanie and I used to talk a lot. When we were little, we shared a room. At night when our parents thought we were asleep, we would sneak out of bed and talk. We could talk in the dark without the lights on, using our hands to fingerspell words to each other. I always had to remind Stephanie not to make any noise. More than once she gave us away with her laugh. She has a weird gulp-laugh that sounds like she's swallowing air.

Sometimes we read together. My fingers followed hers across the braille book. I thought it was neat that we could read without having a light on. I think I learned to read braille before I could read printed words. But once I learned printed words, braille seemed too slow.

Most of the time we talked about what we would do when we grew up. I wanted to be everything: a spy, an astronaut, a doctor. Stephanie always wanted to be a teacher like Mom.

Stephanie was born deaf. There was damage to her auditory nerve—a birth defect. Her eyesight was never good, but there was a time when Stephanie could see light and shadows. We would get up in the middle of the night and play flashlight tag on the wall. She was about six when she lost her sight totally.

That night, long after I went to bed, Stephanie shuffled into my room. She tickled me, gulp-laughed, then stopped abruptly. "I love you, brother," she signed and said in her nasal voice. She stared at the wall for a long time before she shuffled out again.

How can a guy get any sleep with interruptions like that?

Chapter 6

Friday, I worried Nerd Boy would say something about Stephanie at lunch. Not that Freemont and Stolks didn't know about Stephanie. They both have been to my house tons of times. At first, I think they were scared of her. Then, they just ignored her and lately—well, I just didn't have anyone come around.

I hate talking about her, especially at school, but I lucked out. It was a nerd-free lunch. A nerd-free social studies and gym class, too. Maybe he had stayed home from a severe allergic reaction to sugar.

I beat Mom and Stephanie home from school for a change. I grabbed a can of Mountain Dew and a bag of Chee-tos. I plopped on the couch and munched away. Ahhh! Peace! No one pawing at me, wanting me to share.

I heard the automatic garage door go up. My moment of peace was about to end. I shoved as many Chee-tos into my mouth as I could and threw the bag back into the pantry. I brushed the crumbs from my face and wiped my hands on my jeans.

I didn't fool anyone. Ricky burst through the door. "Hi, buddy," he said, giving me five. He stopped, tilted his head to one side, and said, "I smell Chee-tos!"

Stephanie clomped in, sniffed, and put her fingers to my mouth and hands, searching to see if I still had the Chee-tos.

She clunked to the pantry, grabbed the bag, and shuffled off to her room. Ricky followed her screaming, "I want some! Stephanie! Give me some."

"Already?" Mom asked as she came in the back door with two bags of groceries. "There's more in the car," she said, putting the bags on the counter and going down the hall to referee.

Why did I get stuck with all the work? I was too tired to argue about it.

The Chee-tos battle continued at dinner as Stephanie and Ricky fought over everything. We had tacos. Stephanie kept putting her hand on Ricky's plate and stealing pieces of cheese and taco meat. Poor kid.

She ate with her mouth open and smacked her food. She bit into her taco and a bunch of bright orange taco grease dripped down her chin and onto her plate. I hate sitting across from her.

Dad asked about Stephanie's test scores.

"I'm afraid she didn't do so well," Mom said.

"Oh," Dad replied.

"I think the school board has decided she would be better off in Boston," Mom said with a sigh.

"I don't know, Maggie," Dad said. "Maybe they have a point."

Mom's whole body froze. Her eyes riveted to my dad. Mom and Dad both looked at me, then at each other, and continued eating as though nothing had happened. They didn't fool me. I knew what that look meant: *Don't argue in front of the kids.*

Later that night after Ricky was asleep and Stephanie was in her room getting ready for bed, Mom and Dad went into Dad's study and locked the door. I pretended to watch TV, but I turned the volume down real low.

I couldn't hear much. Dad kept saying stuff like "You've done your best." Mom wanted Stephanie to stay here so she could have a *normal* family life.

She had to be kidding. Where had she been for the last ten years? A *normal* family life? The Parsons household was about as far from normal as you could get!

Then they started yelling at each other. Mom and Dad argue now and then, but I had never heard them yell at each other. I crept back to the couch and turned up the TV.

Chapter 7

Just my luck. As if being grounded for the weekend wasn't enough, the schedule for the YMCA Baseball Pony League clinics and tryouts arrived the same day as the pink slips from school. Both were addressed TO THE PARENTS OF MICHAEL PARSONS.

"Totally out of the question" is how Mom started the conversation.

"But, Mom . . ."

"You know the rules. You have to maintain a C average to participate in sports. You're failing math."

"I'm not failing."

She glared at me.

"I'm getting a D," I reminded her.

She breathed in deeply and slowly like she might breathe out fire at any moment.

"I'm getting a D right now, but that's only because of fractions," I said. "Besides, baseball is in the summer. School will be out."

"But baseball *practice* is in the spring and school will be *in*."

"I still have three weeks to pull up my grade."

"Three weeks" was all Mom said.

Chapter 8

The only time I got out of the house all weekend was to go to church on Sunday morning. We go to Trinity Presbyterian Church. It's the church that looks like a big gray castle on Elm Street.

I stretched out on the living-room floor Sunday morning reading the sports page and the comics. Maybe if I acted as if I weren't supposed to go to church, I might get to stay home. Stephanie was ready hours before she needed to be. She shuffled into the living room, stepped on the paper, and tripped over me. She reached down and felt my head and hooted, "MY-Y-Y-Y-Y." She patted my head as if I were a dog as she stepped over me and sat on the couch.

Stephanie *loves* church. She loves getting dressed up. She loves the music. She loves everything.

Today she was wearing a blue flowered dress and black patent leather shoes. She loves the feel of patent leather. She felt her shoes over and over again. When she felt a smudge on the toe of her right shoe, she took the shoe from her foot and clomped to the kitchen with one shoe off and one shoe on. She made a strange peg-leg sound as she clomped through the kitchen to the sink.

My cousin Tiffany took tap dance lessons when she was small. We had made a special trip to Kentucky just to see her dance recital. Mom explained tap dancing to Stephanie.

Tiffany let Stephanie feel the black patent leather tap shoes. Stephanie felt the shiny, smooth tops with the big bows for ties and the hard metal taps underneath. Stephanie knelt down in the rehearsal hall with her forearms flat on the shiny wooden floor as Tiffany tapped around her. Stephanie laughed as if the vibrations tickled her.

Ever since the Kentucky trip, Stephanie had insisted on having patent leather shoes. Tiffany gave up tap years ago and is now more interested in horses and boys, but Stephanie still wears the shoes. Not many fifteen-year-olds wear patent leather shoes. Even though Stephanie has the body of a nine-year-old, she definitely has the feet of a fifteen-year-old. It's getting harder and harder to find patent leather shoes in her size.

Stephanie must have been thinking of Tiffany and the dance recital when she returned from the kitchen because she did a little tap step on the rug. The dance steps made her smile as if she were onstage.

Stephanie sat on the couch and went through her purse, making sure her Kleenex was folded just right. She kept running her hand along the edge of her skirt, feeling the lace and straightening it where it was slightly wrinkled. She opened her watch and felt the braille numbers and hooted for us to hurry.

Mom rushed into the living room to look for Ricky's shoes, which had disappeared again. "Michael, it's getting late. You better hurry."

"But I'm grounded," I reminded her.

She didn't say anything. She just glared at me. I didn't think I should push it. I might end up being grounded until I'm eighteen years old.

But I didn't exactly hurry to my room to get dressed, either.

"Michael, hurry up," she called from the living room fifteen minutes later. She was searching under chairs and beds for Ricky's shoes. "Honestly, Ricky, I think I should treat you like a horse and nail your shoes on you."

"Here they are, Mom," I called. Ricky had kicked them off in my room.

"Bring them with you! He can put them on in the car. Hurry up or we'll be late."

What's the big deal? We're always late to church. Today we managed to get there before the end of the entrance hymn. Dad carried Ricky, who finally had his shoes laced on. Mom followed with Stephanie on her arm. I tiptoed in behind everyone. Even with the organ blasting, you could hear the sharp click of Stephanie's heels as she clunked down the church aisle. I swear everyone turned to look at us.

Stephanie loves music. Don't ask me why. She can't hear it, but she can feel the deep notes of the organ vibrating the pews. As soon as we sat down, she had her hands on everyone's throats to make sure we were singing. First, she felt the hymnbooks and then our throats as if between the two she could decipher the hymn we were singing. Then she hummed along, not just off-key but totally—off.

Everyone for three rows in front of us turned around to see where the noise was coming from. When they realized it was Stephanie, they turned back and pretended not to notice.

When Mrs. Hatwell, the organist, finished playing, she gave my mom this pitiful look.

Mom makes us take turns signing the sermon to Stephanie. Today was my turn. I hate it. Reverend Gardner uses such hard words. It's hard to listen to what he's saying, think of a way of paraphrasing it into signs I know, and sign it to Stephanie. I always end up leaving out a whole chunk somewhere along the line. Today was one of his *long* sermons. I couldn't wait for him to finish. After the sermon, he launched into this long thank-you for all the committee members of last week's craft bazaar. We didn't go, and Stephanie didn't know any of the people he was talking about, so I signed "finished" and pushed her hands back toward her lap.

But Reverend Gardner yammered on and Stephanie, confused, grew restless. She reached over and felt my throat. I pushed her hand away. Stephanie plopped a hymnbook in my lap and signed "sing" to me. I folded the book up and put it back in the book rack. She grunted, shook her head and got it out again, and slapped it open on my lap. Then she put two fingers on my throat and waited expectantly. Her eyes flitted back into her head and she had that smile on her face. I moved her hand to my chin and shook my head no. The whole time this was happening, I could see Julia Patterson out of the corner of my right eye. She was sitting one row up and across the aisle. She looked back at us and whispered to her little brother. Every time I caught her eyes on us, my cheeks burned bright red.

I handed Stephanie her braille prayer book, but she shoved it back in my direction. Stephanie knew that after the sermon we always sang as they passed the collection plate.

"Nooooooooo!" she hooted. Her nasal voice reverberated off the rafters.

It took Reverend Gardner a whole twenty seconds to get back into his thank-yous. The rest of the congregation squirmed with discomfort as they tried to pretend they hadn't heard anything. Julia Patterson clamped her hand over her mouth to keep from laughing.

Mom shot a look at me as she signed something to

Stephanie. I don't know what it was, but it calmed Stephanie down and she sat laughing softly with an "I won the lottery" smile on her face. Mom glared at me through the rest of the service.

"What did I do?" I mouthed at her. She just glared and glared.

I shrugged my shoulders and looked the other way.

Mrs. Randolph didn't help. This lady has her nose in everything. She has to be real old, but her hair is all one color—shoe-polish brown. She wears bright lipstick and makes kissy faces when she talks. She talks to everyone— even Dad—like they're in nursery school.

"Oh, Maggie. How are you," she said in her singsongy voice. "And how is Stephanie, the sweet dear." She held her hand out toward Stephanie, but didn't touch her.

"You are so *won*derful with her," her voice dripped sweet. "And she's getting so grown up. Twelve, isn't it?"

"Actually, Stephanie is fifteen, almost sixteen."

"Fifteen already! Oh, the years *do* pass."

"Stephanie has her own special prayer book, just like me. See," Ricky said. He stood on tiptoe and shoved his prayer book into Mrs. Randolph's face. "I have a monkey named Peanuts. Mom wouldn't let me bring him. Mom said monkeys aren't allowed in church. That's OK, Peanuts is taking a nap in the car," Ricky said with a nod.

Mrs. Randolph oozed out some sickeningly sweet laughter and ruffled Ricky's thick blond curls. "What a precious child," she cackled.

Meanwhile, Stephanie was standing right in the middle of the coatroom with that smile plastered on her face. She looked so excited and happy—like it was her first visit to Disney World. Everyone was avoiding her like she was poisonous. Now and then, someone bumped into her and she'd gulp-laugh. If no one bumped into her for a while, she'd reach out and touch people as they passed. People always look startled. Then they'll smile nervously and look around to see if anyone is watching them.

I could tell Mom was still mad by the way she held her lips together. When the car began rolling, she started in on me.

"Michael James! I am so ashamed! And in the house of God, no less!"

You would have thought I robbed the collection plate!

"What did I do?"

"Provoked your sister."

"What? I provoked *her*?"

I looked at Stephanie, who was staring blankly out the window. She had her hand spread flat on the windowpane as if she could feel the scenery as it passed by.

"She wanted me to sing during the sermon. What did you want me to do?" I knew my face was turning red.

Mom didn't answer.

"Well . . ." I demanded. "What am I supposed to do?"

"That's enough," Dad said. "I will not allow you to be disrespectful. You'd better watch your step, son, or you'll find yourself grounded . . . basketball and all."

"But . . . ," I sputtered.

"NOW," he bellowed.

I fixed my face in a scowl, folded my arms and scrunched down in the seat. *That shows how much he knows,* I thought. *Basketball was over nearly a month ago.*

Chapter 9

I never thought I would look forward to going to school, but after being stuck in the house all weekend doing chores for Mom, I even looked forward to going to Ms. Rothchild's class.

Dad had an early morning meeting, so I didn't have a ride to school. While I was still in bed, he stopped by my room with his briefcase in his hand.

"You're on your own this morning," he reminded me. "Better get moving."

By the time I made it to school, the first bell had already rung and everyone was running for class. Davidson chased Willowby past me, bumping into people on both sides of the hall. They slowed down to a fast walk in front of the hall monitor and broke into a run again going around the corner. Willowby slammed right into Julia Patterson, sending her books skidding across the floor in every direction.

A big smile spread across my face. I couldn't think of anyone who deserved it more.

"Hey, watch it, jerk!" she screamed after Willowby, who disappeared into a sea of people.

"Oh, Mic." She smiled when she saw me. "Could you please pick up my math book?" She scooped up the other books around her.

I acted like I didn't hear her.

Did that discourage her? No. She hopped to the math book, picked it up, and chased after me.

"I saw you with your sister at church yesterday. What's her name?" she asked, running after me. I was walking as fast as I could.

I reached my locker. Freemont had struck again. The lock was on backward. I knelt down to work the combination upside down and backward. Now I know why the teachers warn us not to give out our combinations even to our best friends.

"What's her name?" Julia pretended to think hard. "Stephanie, isn't it?"

"If you knew, why did you ask?"

"Oh, you were wonderful with her. You do all that hand talk. I think that's fabulous."

My first try at the lock failed. I tugged and jiggled it, hoping it would open. No luck. I groaned and started again.

"My mother says your mother has the patience of a saint . . . a real miracle worker . . . you know, like Anne Sullivan with Helen Keller in *The Miracle Worker,*" she babbled on.

I opened the locker and tossed my social studies book in the bottom.

"How are you doing, Mic?" Freemont asked. He slapped me so hard on the back, I could feel where each of his five fingers hit me.

"Are you proposing to Julia? I saw you down on your knees." Freemont grinned.

Julia started giggling hysterically.

"Oh, David. You know Mic and I are just friends."

I rolled my eyes.

"We go to the same church, don't we?" she said.

"Going to church together, huh?" Freemont said with a

smirk. He put his arm over my shoulder. "Walking down the aisle together, huh?"

He jumped out of the way as I slammed my locker.

"Well, can I be best man . . . huh, Mic?"

Before I could say anything, Julia started cackling. "Oh, David! You're so funny." Cackle. Cackle.

"Yeah, real funny." I made a face at him.

"David," she said, trying to catch up with us as we hurried down the hallway. "Do you know Mic's sister, Stephanie? You know, the one who's deaf and blind?"

"Sure," Freemont called back to her. "Stolks and I have watched her run into walls for years."

We both laughed.

"David," she said, "don't you think it's just marvelous how she gets around? And she does things almost like normal people."

We looked at each other. I rolled my eyes.

"Amy Burnhart says you belong to her swim club and Stephanie gets in the water and swims and everything," she said.

"Even my dog can do that," Freemont sneered.

I wondered if she would ever shut up. We were almost to Ms. Rothchild's room.

"And Mic," she continued, "he's so wonderful with her . . . doing all that hand stuff and all, to talk to her."

I pushed open the door to Rothchild's class.

"Bye, Julia," Freemont called back to her. "Mic will meet you at your locker later."

"Why did you say that?"

"Anything I can do to bring you two lovebirds together," he said, grinning.

"If Rothchild wasn't watching, I'd pound you."

"Ooh, I'm scared."

Lucky for Freemont the bell rang.

I don't know which was worse: being grounded all weekend or having to talk about fractions first thing on Monday morning.

This morning, Ms. Rothchild talked about mixed numbers and improper fractions.

To me, all fractions are *improper*. I paged ahead in the book. Fifty more pages of fractions to go. That had to mean at least a quarter of the book was on fractions. I couldn't believe it. I had actually used a fraction. But that was easy. I knew what a quarter or a half of something was. It was when I had to add, subtract, multiply, and divide fractions that I got into trouble.

"Yes, Michael?" Ms. Rothchild called on me when I raised my hand during our work time.

"When's our next test?"

"A week from today."

Everyone groaned.

"On a Monday?" someone complained.

It didn't matter if it were on Christmas. I still wouldn't understand what I was supposed to do.

Chapter 10

I scanned the lunchroom for any sign of Nerd Boy as I ate my pizza in big bites. I was in a bad mood. Math hadn't just ruined a *fraction* of my day; it had ruined my *whole* day. The last thing I needed was Nerd Boy showing up and talking about Stephanie. If I saw him coming, I'd bail. I shoved in the last bite of pizza and washed it down with a carton of milk.

No Nerd Boy.

Lunch was almost over. As I ate my dessert, I started to breathe easier.

Maybe Nerd Boy is sick, I thought. *Maybe he's found someone else to bug.* That's when the paperboy's sack fell with a thud across from me.

Stolks scooted out of the way.

"Baseball tryouts are in three weeks," Nerd Boy said after he attacked the lasagna on his tray. "What position are you going to try out for?"

"*You* play baseball?" I asked.

"Pitcher," he said, nodding.

I looked at him. He was a skinny, string-bean, four-eyed geek. No! This kid could *not* be a baseball player.

Nerd Boy was a pitcher? The thought boggled my mind. I simply couldn't see him on the mound zinging a fastball across home plate. I couldn't even imagine him in a baseball uniform. And what kind of socks does a sock-collecting nerd baseball pitcher wear?

The only way I could possibly see Vernon Chortle on a baseball team was as a manager. *That* I could see. He would be hunched over the scorekeeper's book diligently recording every statistic. He probably had a computer at home that could calculate every stat—all the usual ones plus weather conditions and the astrological signs of each player so he knew precisely where, how, and when to strike players out. The nerd's approach to baseball.

The thought of Nerd Boy at tryouts and me at home nearly killed me. I tried to think of a way to get Mom to change her mind as I walked home from school. It was hopeless.

"Want to hit a few this afternoon?"

I must have jumped three feet.

"Sorry, Four-Twelve. I didn't mean to scare you."

Nerd Boy had walked up behind me and was now walking beside me.

"My name is Mic," I told him.

"I know."

"Where's your bike?"

"Walked today. Wanna hit a few? My dad will be home in an hour and he can help us practice."

The thought of meeting the Nerd's dad wasn't appealing.

I shrugged. Then I thought about him as the Wonderful Wizard Baseball Computer. If he could calculate hitters, he might be able to calculate pitchers. It wouldn't hurt to find out.

"I guess so."

"See you in about an hour then," he said as he played

around with his watch. Then he started speed-walking, pulling ahead of me. He walked like he ate—fast! He was nearly a block ahead of me by the time we turned onto our court. A skinny, off-white figure with a strange straight-legged walk. Only a sliver of neon orange showed between his shoes and his pants.

I immediately regretted agreeing to go to Nerd Boy's house. I would have backed out, but Mom was in the middle of some cooking project and wanted me to help. I figured getting out of the house was getting out of the house.

From the outside, Chortle's house at the end of the cul-de-sac looked like any normal house. But I figured the inside would be like a mad scientist's lab. It wasn't until a nice-looking woman answered the door that I realized I hadn't met anyone else in Nerd Boy's family since they moved in. I hadn't even seen any of them.

"You must be Mic." She smiled. "Vernon has told me so much about you." She stuck out her hand to shake mine. She looked nice—like a TV mom.

I shook her hand, wondering what Nerd Boy knew about me to tell her.

"Great timing! I just took the last batch of cookies out of the oven," she said. The house smelled delicious.

"Please thank your mother for lending me a cup of sugar last week. I have a plate of cookies and a cup of sugar to send back with you."

My stomach growled in approval.

"Vernon, Mic is here," she called up the stairs.

"He's early," we heard from the far corners of the house.

Mrs. Chortle must have heard my stomach growling. She ran back to the kitchen and returned with another plate of cookies.

"Go on up," she said, handing me the plate. "Vernon's room is the last door on the left."

I couldn't resist sneaking a cookie and cramming it in my mouth before I reached the top of the stairs. It was still warm and moist, and it melted in my mouth. Mmm-m-m-m-m-m-m.

"Can I have one?" a voice said from behind. I jumped so high I nearly threw the cookies to the ceiling. These Chortles must be specially trained in the art of sneaking up on people.

I didn't say anything, but she took one from the plate anyway. "I'm Angela, Vern's sister. I'm nine and in the fourth grade," she said, pushing her mousy brown hair back behind her ears. She didn't look nerdy at all.

A loud blast of classical-type music rocked the house, followed by a woman screaming. Then Mrs. Chortle yowled, too.

"Is your mom OK?" I asked.

"I doubt it." Angela rolled her eyes.

"What's that noise?" I asked.

"Opera," Angela said, like it was some disease.

From the yowling I heard going on in the kitchen, it sounded like a painful one.

"Keep it down. I'm on the phone," said a voice from the room at the top of the stairs.

A girl with long, beautiful hair was lying across the bed talking on the phone. Her legs were long and beautiful, too.

"You're always on the phone," Angela said, rolling her eyes.

The girl got up from the bed carrying the phone with her and walked to the door. She gave us a dirty look before she slammed the door in our faces.

"That's Jessica. She's sixteen." Angela sighed as if that piece of information explained everything.

The last door on the left was closed. It had signs all over it. The biggest said

KNOCK BEFORE ENTERING!

The rest all said DANGER or KEEP OUT (THIS MEANS YOU!). There were skulls and crossbones everywhere.

Angela was still on my heels. I decided I'd better knock just in case Nerd Boy's nuclear attack socks were armed today.

Angela flattened herself against the wall next to the door. I knocked three times. Angela put her finger to her mouth and motioned for me to be quiet.

"Come on in, Four-Twelve."

I turned the knob and the door squeaked open. He was probably dissecting something.

"You can get lost, Angela," Nerd Boy said before the door was even halfway open.

Angela groaned and stomped off down the hall.

"Come on in, Four-Twelve," Vern said again. He wasn't dissecting anything. He was sorting through baseball cards. "Good. Cookies," he said, taking the plate from my hands.

My mouth dropped open. Never in my wildest dreams had I envisioned a room like this. It was unbelievable.

Chapter 11

"Wow!" I said.

The alarm on his watch started beeping.

"You're early. This is when you were supposed to get here. Dad will be home anytime," he said as he reset the alarm.

I couldn't move. I forgot for a moment that I was standing in Nerd Boy's room. In fact, I forgot all about Nerd Boy. I thought perhaps I had died and gone to heaven. Baseball heaven.

The whole wall above his bed was covered with a plastic grid and filled with baseball cards. Hundreds of them. They were divided by teams: American League, National League, and a special section for All-Stars.

The wall across from his bed had floor-to-ceiling shelves. On the bottom four shelves were clear boxes filled with even more baseball cards. The top four shelves held trophies and pictures. Big trophies. Small trophies. Pitching trophies. Batting trophies. Team pictures. Single pictures. Action pictures. Posed pictures. Signed and autographed pictures of baseball stars. There was an Ozzie Smith and a Mark McGwire. Was this real or was I dreaming? I forgot about sock collections, computers, mad scientist labs, and dissecting small animals.

The only weird thing in the whole room was on the back

of the door. There were three maps: a map of how to get to the school, a layout of the school, and a map of the cul-de-sac. Each house had the house number written in big red letters. Scrawled beneath my house were the words *"Kid in my class."*

By the time I unglued my eyes from all the stuff in the room, the cookies were gone. "Dad's home," he said, trotting out of the room and down the stairs.

I followed him in a daze.

As Mr. Chortle came in the front door, I saw his car in the driveway. How did I miss seeing that this past week? A laser-blue Mustang convertible. Wow!

"Give me a chance to change," Mr. Chortle said as I caught up to Nerd Boy. "You must be Mic," he said, shaking my hand. "You guys go out and limber up. I'll be right out."

Mr. Chortle looked like a normal, average dad. Better than the average dad—no glasses, no bald spot, and not chubby at all. Maybe Nerd Boy was adopted.

"Come on," Nerd Boy called. He was already outside and motioned for me to join him.

I looked for my jacket to put on and realized I had never taken it off. Nerd Boy put his glove on his right hand and tossed a ball in my direction. A southpaw! My stomach twisted in a knot. I always had trouble hitting off left-handed pitchers.

"Wow. Nice glove," I said.

"A Rawlings," he said. "Dad bought it for me right before the playoffs last year."

From across the grass, I could see how shiny and new it was. I could almost smell the leather.

I looked down at the glove on my hand. It was four years old. It lost its shine after I left it out in the rain when I was eleven. Mine smelled more like sweat socks.

As we tossed the ball back and forth, I started to move around and wake up from the daze I had been in. The cool March air stung my lungs. Now that I was out of "Baseball Heaven," I remembered who I was dealing with. Nerd Boy tossed a hard one. Neon orange flashed from his ankles.

I'm not a power hitter, but I have a good eye. My first Little League coach had taught me to meet the ball and not try to smash it every time. I was a pretty good place hitter.

I don't know where Nerd Boy had gotten all his trophies, but I was confident he couldn't strike me out.

"OK, guys," Mr. Chortle called as he joined us in the backyard. "Let's shake those old cobwebs loose."

Mr. Chortle put us through a bunch of drills. First, he hit a few grounders our way.

Nerd Boy had great hands! And he's fast! After fielding grounders, Mr. Chortle pitched to us.

"Mic," he said when we finished, "you have a good eye. I bet you don't strike out much."

"Only seven strikeouts last year," I said.

"Bet you get a lot of walks, too," he said.

"Yup, more than anyone else on my team."

"Just remember," he said with a pat on my back, "a batter with a good eye and bat control is as good as a power slugger—better, usually."

"Let's see how the old arm is," he said to Nerd Boy, who stood ready to pitch to me. With all the confidence in the world, I raised my bat and stared Nerd Boy down.

Chapter 12

"Dinner's ready!" Mom called from the kitchen.

The door to my bedroom was open and I had been listening to the noise in the kitchen since I got home from the Chortles' an hour ago. Something weird was up.

"Mic! Paul!" Mom called. "Dinner."

I heard Dad click off the TV evening news. "My goodness," he said as he walked into the kitchen. "What's the special occasion?"

I didn't hear how Mom answered or if she answered at all.

I didn't move. I didn't even try. I felt frozen. I wished I could melt into the bed and disappear from the face of the earth.

"Ricky, go find your brother. Tell him dinner is ready," I heard Mom say.

Ricky must have jumped from the stool in the kitchen, because there was a big thud followed by the scurrying of little feet. I heard him coming down the hall. I didn't move.

"Are you taking a nap?" Ricky asked when he got to my bedroom door. He had Peanuts with him.

I didn't answer.

"Mic? You asleep?" Ricky called from the door.

"Mom," Ricky called when I didn't answer. I knew he was going to tell her I was asleep.

"I'm not asleep," I forced my mouth to say.

"Why are the lights out?" he asked, coming into the room, dragging Peanuts by the tail. He plopped on the bed next to me and made Peanuts jump up and down on my back.

I shrugged.

"Ricky! Mic! Everything's getting cold."

"Come on! Dinner! We made homemade pizza!" He grabbed me by the hand and tried to pull me from the bed.

I wasn't hungry. Not even for pizza. Maybe I would never eat again.

"Ricky? Michael?" Mom called again. "Now I've lost them both."

I heard Stephanie's shrill nasal "REE-E-E-E-E-E-E-E! MY-Y-Y-Y-Y-Y-Y-Y!"

"Ricky! Michael! Let's go," Dad added.

"Come on," Ricky said at the same time and pulled on my hand again.

I figured I'd better get up before they called out the National Guard. "OK. OK. I'm coming," I told Ricky. "You go on. I'll be right there."

"PIZZZZZZZZA!" Ricky bellowed like he was Tarzan and Peanuts was Cheetah.

"What's going on?" I asked when I reached the kitchen door.

Candlelight flickered in the dark kitchen. A red-and-white checkered tablecloth covered the table. A delicious smell filled the room. A Chicago-style deep-dish pizza sat in the center of the table.

Stephanie looked toward me and said, "PPPEEEEEEE DDDDDDAAAAA!" Her smile stretched from ear to ear.

"Paul, you may do the honors," Mom said, passing the pizza cutter and pie server to Dad like he was going to carve a Thanksgiving turkey or something.

As Dad cut the pizza, Mom turned on the tape recorder. Italian accordion music spilled into the room. I felt as if we were in the little café from the love scene in *Lady and the Tramp*. Mom held Stephanie's hand to the speaker and then moved her hands in and out as if Stephanie were playing an accordion. Stephanie giggled. Her eyes flitted back into her head.

Dad lifted out fat, thick slices of pizza that dripped with sauce and cheese. "Ladies first," he said, serving Mom and Stephanie.

"What's going on?" I asked again, as Dad plopped a big piece of pizza on my plate.

"Pizza," Ricky answered. "We made it. Mom helped, but Stephanie and I put the dough in the pan all by ourselves."

"I *know* it's pizza, Ricky," I said.

"What's the special occasion, Maggie?" Dad asked.

"Can't I just make a special meal without a reason?"

"This must have taken hours," Dad said, cutting away a piece for himself.

"It's just been awhile since I cooked with the kids." Mom took a big bite of her pizza. Chicago-style pizza is so thick, you can't eat it with your fingers like thin flat pizza. You have to use a knife and fork. "MaryJane loaned me her pizza-making kit. I thought the kids would get a kick out of it. You know how Stephanie likes to cook and this might be . . . well . . . It's been a long time."

When Stephanie and I were small, we used to cook together all the time. Stephanie had her own braille cookbook and a set of measuring cups to help her measure. I couldn't remember the last time we had worked together on anything.

Dad said that since the three of them had worked so hard on dinner, he and I would be happy to clean up. Of course, he didn't ask me first, but I wasn't in a hurry to start my math homework.

I didn't know how much I had enjoyed the candlelight and music until Dad shut off the tape player, blew out the candle, and turned on the lights. The room was transformed back to our normal, messy kitchen. There was flour every-where.

I think it would have been easier just to hose down the whole room, but we cleaned it with only a cloth and sponge mop. It took nearly an hour. When we finished, I grabbed a couple of Mrs. Chortle's cookies and settled in front of the tube.

"Homework done?" Dad asked, ruining a perfect moment.

I went to my room and opened my math book to page 247. Our assignment for the night: thirty-six problems. I knew I would strike out on the problems just as quickly as I had struck out from Nerd Boy's pitches. Never in a million years would I have believed I would strike out so miserably from a guy who looked so nerdy. He must have pitched over fifty pitches to me and I couldn't hit one. Not ONE. I man-aged to get a piece of the ball only three times. I popped up all three times.

I looked at the math problems in front of me. By the looks of it, I wasn't going to bring up my math grade anyway, so I wasn't even going to be able to try out for the team.

I was watching my baseball life flash before my eyes when I heard Dad's and Mom's voices from Dad's study.

"I know what you are doing, Maggie," Dad said. "Don't beat yourself up like this."

"I don't know what you mean."

Neither did I.

I moved closer to the door to listen.

"Tonight's dinner. It's OK if you are doing it for the right reasons. But you don't have to prove anything to me or yourself or anybody."

"What are you implying?"

Yes. What was he implying?

"I saw what came in the mail today."

I wasn't sure, but I thought I heard Mom sobbing.

"I feel like such a failure."

"You're not a failure. You have done a beautiful job raising and educating your daughter, but now it's time to let go."

Chapter 13

Stolks, Freemont, and I started playing baseball together when we were in kindergarten. OK, it wasn't *real* baseball—it was T-ball—but close enough.

Over the years, we played different positions. Because of his size, Stolks seemed natural at catcher. I played different infield positions before I settled in at second base. Freemont spent most of his years in the outfield. This past season, he played center field. He didn't really have the arm for center field, but Coach thought he would grow into the position.

The three of us have spent more time playing baseball together than doing anything else. We've been through practice drills, tryouts, blowouts, and rain-outs. Baseball is our language. I thought I could tell these guys anything. Especially, anything that had to do with baseball. Until now.

What should I say to Freemont and Stolks? Should I tell them how pathetic I was? Should I tell them how great Nerd Boy was? They would never believe me. How much would Nerd Boy say at lunch? Maybe I should just keep quiet. But I couldn't chance it. I figured it would be better to say something to the guys than for Vern to surprise them.

"Guess where I went after school yesterday?" I asked Freemont and Stolks between the first bell and first hour. "Nerd Boy's house."

Immediately, I wished I hadn't said anything.

"I knew you two were getting chummy. Quick, Stolks! Check out his socks." Freemont tossed his books at Stolks, who dropped the books he was carrying in order to catch Freemont's books. Freemont lunged for my pant legs and pulled them up to my knees. "Just as I suspected—collector-quality socks!"

"Ha-ha. Very funny," I said. I pulled my pant legs from his grip and walked down the hall toward Ms. Rothchild's class.

"Watch out, Stolksie! Tomorrow Mic here will probably be wearing white jeans," Freemont said with a big grin.

Stolks laughed as he gathered up his books from the floor and stacked them on top of Freemont's books.

"Look! Look!" Freemont pointed at me as I walked down the hall. A few people turned around and stared.

"What?" I asked. My face was bright red.

"The WALK." Freemont doubled over with laughter. "He's already got the WALK." Freemont straightened up and did a pretty good imitation of Nerd Boy's quick-paced, straight-legged speed walk.

He zoomed down the hall with his big nose shoved in the air. He walked right past Julia Patterson.

"W-w-w-wait," Stolks called after him. "Your books."

Stolks forgot all about me as he chased after Freemont.

"That David!" Julia laughed, patting my arm like we were sharing some gigantic joke. She didn't know the joke was on me. "Isn't he a *scream*?"

At that precise moment, Freemont turned the corner and ran into the real Nerd Boy. Nerd Boy fell backward on his news carrier's bag with a thud. Freemont fell on top of him. Stolks, who just caught up with Freemont, tripped over their tangled legs and went down, sending his double load of books sprawling across the hall.

I couldn't help laughing.

Julia, who hadn't seen the collision, thought I was laughing with her and took the opportunity to move her hand from my arm, pat me on the back, and give me a little hug.

I shuddered and pushed Julia away.

Thank God, the bell rang.

As soon as she took attendance, Ms. Rothchild asked us to pass our homework papers to the person in back of us to grade in class. I hated grading homework in class. The only thing worse than passing papers is working out problems on the board. Today I had to pass my paper to Cynthia Miles. Not only is Cynthia good in math, she's a friend of Julia's. Double yuck.

I wasn't surprised when Cynthia passed the paper back with a big fat zero on the top of the page. *"Try to be a little neater,"* she had written in perfect printing below the big zero—like *she* was the teacher. By noon Julia would know about my terrible math grade and would be begging to help me study.

"For those of you who are having trouble with fractions, I will be having a peer tutoring session tonight after school," Ms. Rothchild said.

I'm not sure, but I think she was looking directly at me.

After last night's great homemade pizza, I decided to take my chances with the regular hot lunch meal instead of the usual slice of pizza I had for lunch every day. They were serving grilled cheese today, which usually isn't too bad. But I think the fruit cocktail might have been left over from when my parents had been in junior high school.

"Even eating like Nerd Boy. I knew it would happen," Freemont said when I put my tray on the table. He was halfway through his hoagie.

I didn't answer. Sometimes it's best not to give Freemont any ammunition. Freemont could turn *anything* you said around.

"Well, did you see them?" he asked me.

"What?"

"The socks." Freemont turned to Stolks. "How many pairs did he say he had?"

"Three hundred and eighty-four," Stolks said through a bite full of ham sandwich. "No! It was three hundred and eighty-two. Wasn't it?"

"Well, what was it? Three hundred and eighty-two? Three hundred and eighty-four? Did you count them?"

I shook my head.

"You were in the room with probably the largest sock collection in Illinois—maybe the largest sock collection in the world—and you didn't even count them?!"

Freemont definitely knew how to make you feel real stupid.

"Didn't see one pair," I said.

Actually, I had forgotten totally about the socks. I wondered where Nerd Boy stored them. Maybe they were in the closet. Maybe he kept them in plastic storage bags. Maybe he had little sock hangers for them. I wish I had taken time to look for them.

I looked up and saw Nerd Boy walking toward the table.

He must have seen me look at his ankles. There is no way he could have heard what we were talking about from that far away. When he got to the table, he plopped his tray down and pushed his news carrier's bag totally under the table. He raised his foot and pulled up his pant leg.

He was wearing purple socks with gray shark fins swimming around his ankles. "I call this pair Shark Attack. They are in the top ten of my all-time favorite socks."

Freemont fell forward on the table in a convulsion of laughter. "You *name* your socks?"

Nerd Boy sat down and started eating his grilled cheese as if naming socks wasn't anything unusual. He ate the crust of his grilled cheese sandwich like he was eating an ear of corn, taking continual small bites around the edge of the sandwich till there was no crust left. He was left holding the small center piece of grilled cheese, which he popped into his mouth and swallowed without hardly chewing it at all.

Freemont straightened up, put on a serious face, and leaned forward. "I heard Mic was over at your place yesterday."

"Yeah, we were getting ready for baseball tryouts."

"Yeah. Yeah." Freemont nodded like he knew all about it. "Mic says that you are pretty wicked on the ball field."

I hadn't had a chance to tell Freemont how good Nerd Boy was.

"Four-Twelve's not bad, either," Nerd Boy said. "You need to choke up on the bat more," he said to me as he shoveled in a spoonful of fruit cocktail.

I was kind of surprised to hear he thought I was good at all after my horrible showing at the plate. "You really think I need to choke up on the bat more?" I asked him.

"Yeah. Just a little. Actually, you don't need much adjustment at all. You have a good level swing and a great eye."

"I couldn't seem to hit off you," I admitted.

"You were just tense. Left-handers make you nervous, don't they?"

"Yeah."

"They make lots of people nervous—that's why I've been so successful. But you can learn to hit off left-handers."

The way he said it made it sound like he knew some secret formula. He shoveled in his last spoonful of fruit cocktail. "Just don't tell everybody," he said as he wiped fruit cocktail syrup from his chin with the back of his hand. "I like striking out people. Don't think we can practice tonight because of the weather, but maybe we can get together later in the week."

"Yeah."

"Later, Four-Twelve," he said getting up from the table.

"The name is Mic."

"I know. I like Four-Twelve better."

He went to the trash can, dumped his garbage, stacked his tray, and walked away without looking back.

"I can't believe this," Freemont said. His mouth was hanging open. "Can you believe this, Stolksie?"

"Uh-uh." Stolks shook his head. He put a whole Chips Ahoy in his mouth.

"I was kidding before, but you two are really getting chummy, aren't you!"

"Come on, Freemont. We were just warming up for the baseball tryouts. He lives down the street. It's not a big deal."

"Apparently, it is! 'Choke up on the bat, Four-Twelve'; 'Left-handers make you nervous, Four-Twelve'!"

"His dad used to be a baseball coach. You know it wouldn't hurt for you to practice before tryouts. Do you want to come over after school and hit a few?"

"Gee, I don't know, Four-Twelve. The Wizard of Nerds seems to think the weather's not right."

"It's not *that* bad."

"Stolks and I will sit this one out. Come on, Stolks." Freemont pulled at Stolks's T-shirt. Stolks shoved the last few crumbs in his mouth and lumbered off after Freemont.

Chapter 14

I remembered Ms. Rothchild's peer-tutoring session just as I was leaving the building. I didn't know exactly what peer tutoring was, but it might be my last chance to pull my grade up in time for baseball tryouts.

I climbed the stairs to Ms. Rothchild's room two at a time.

"Please put your name on a card and drop it into the red box and grab a seat," Ms. Rothchild told me. "I think there's one in the back."

I couldn't believe it. The room was packed. There were only two seats left. I felt better knowing I wasn't the only one having problems with fractions.

"I realize when information is presented in different ways it is easier to learn," said Ms. Rothchild. "Peer tutoring will allow you to learn the material from one of your peers."

I started looking around the room. Willowby and Davidson were here, I noticed. And that, no—it couldn't be. Penny Parrish? And next to her Cynthia? Cynthia Miles was about the smartest person in our class. What was she doing here? And what was Julia Patterson doing sitting right next to her! I had a feeling I should have looked up the word *peer* before I came. What was Ms. Rothchild saying?

". . . so I've invited some of the better students to help those of you who are having problems. It looks like we have just about the right number of students and peer teachers," she said, shaking up the cards in two separate boxes. "We'll match you guys up, and you can get started with the problems on the board. Cynthia Miles," she read from the card she pulled from the blue box. "And Jason Davidson."

I looked over and saw Julia sitting next to Cynthia. She had her eyes squeezed shut and the fingers on both hands crossed. Ms. Rothchild rattled off another pair of names. And another and another. I didn't like the odds that were shaping up.

Julia looked back at me and waved. I could just hear her squeal with delight if Ms. Rothchild called our names together. I could see her trying to teach me fractions, scooting her chair close to mine, leaning over and touching my hand. I couldn't stand it. I jumped up and walked to the door. "Sorry, Ms. Rothchild! I forgot. I have an orthodontist appointment." I don't know what made me use that excuse, but I made sure not to look at Ms. Rothchild or open my mouth—or she might remember I didn't have braces.

Outside it was cold and rainy. I walked home without pulling up my hood. A steady drizzle pecked at the top of my head. The chapter test was next Monday—three pages of questions I would never be able to answer no matter how much time she gave me.

It started raining harder. I lifted my face to the gray sky. I felt the cold raindrops splash on my face. Ms. Rothchild would never forgive me for walking out on her peer tutoring class. If I asked Mom for help, she would only tell me to "apply myself." There had to be someone—anyone besides Julia Patterson—who could help me.

By the time I turned the corner onto Bixby Court, my hair was matted to my head. Chortle's house came into view. Chortle. Nerd Boy. Sock Freak. Computer Whiz. Yes. Why hadn't I thought of it before? Nerd Boy would be a whiz at math and fractions. And he lived just down the street!

Weird orchestra-type music poured out of the house into the rainy afternoon as soon as Mrs. Chortle opened her front door.

"Mic! You're soaked to the bone," Mrs. Chortle said over the screeching music. She ran from the foyer and returned with a towel. "Here. Dry yourself off. I'll get some hot chocolate for you. Do you like cinnamon rolls?"

I stepped in the door and sniffed. The whole house smelled like cinnamon. I nodded and started drying myself off.

"They'll be out of the oven in a few minutes. Did you lock yourself out of the house? Is your mother not home? Is everything all right, Mic?" she asked.

"No. Fine," I answered, handing her the damp towel back. "I just came to see Ner— Vern."

Angela peered at me from the kitchen door. Her eyes were big. Did I really look that bad?

"Angela, please tell your brother that Mic is here. Mic, come in the kitchen and sit down. I'll get that hot chocolate for you."

I caught a glimpse of myself in the mirror in the hall on the way to the kitchen. I did look kind of pathetic.

"Marshmallows or whipped cream?" Mrs. Chortle asked when the microwave beeped. The stereo was turned up so loud that the dishes rattled in the cupboards. Some woman was still shouting out a song in some foreign language.

"Whipped cream," I said.

Mrs. Chortle expertly plopped a big glob of whipped cream on top of the hot chocolate. It looked like something out of a magazine.

I heard the dryer buzz in the laundry room.

"I'll be right back," Mrs. Chortle said, as if I might get scared if I didn't know.

Angela popped up from behind the bar the moment she left the room.

The woman on the stereo squealed again. I felt like plugging my ears.

"Opera?" I asked Angela.

"Yup." She nodded. "*Madam Butterfly* . . . my parents' favorite." She rolled her eyes.

"Does your mom play that music all the time? How do you stand it?"

"At least I don't have to watch it anymore," she said. "Mom used to work at the Cincinnati Opera. She gave tours and stuff like that. She hasn't found a job yet since we moved, so she's driving us crazy . . . baking and meddling."

Angela tiptoed to the oven, cracked it open, and inhaled. The smell of warm cinnamon was dizzying.

"Actually, the baking's not that bad," she said, licking icing from the edge of the mixing bowl. "But the meddling . . ." She rolled her eyes. "Better be careful or she'll start poking into your life, too. Shh-h-h-h! Here she comes."

Angela ducked behind the counter again as Mrs. Chortle returned with a laundry basket full of towels.

"I know you don't know me very well, Mic," she said as she started folding towels. "But I want you to know if there is any time you need to talk to someone, you can always come to me."

I nodded as I took a sip from the hot chocolate.

"This is very good. Thank you."

Mrs. Chortle waited like she expected me to say something else.

"Thank you," I repeated.

She smiled nervously, wiped her hands on her apron, and went to check the cinnamon rolls in the oven.

Someone tapped at my ankle and I jumped.

"See I told you . . . ," Angela whispered. She had crawled around the counter to where I was sitting.

"I said it would be too wet to play today," Nerd Boy said from the kitchen door.

"Vernon. Sit down. The cinnamon rolls will be out in a second," Mrs. Chortle said, putting a mug in front of him.

Angela popped up right next to me. "Can I have some, too?" Angela whined.

Mrs. Chortle handed her a mug and shooed her out of the room.

Nerd Boy and I sipped at our hot chocolate and watched Mrs. Chortle as she took the cinnamon rolls from the oven and put icing on them. Seconds later she placed a plate of warm, fresh, steaming cinnamon rolls in front of us. The smell alone left me drooling.

"Just what we need on a cold, dreary day. If you'll excuse me, I'll take a plate to Angela and Jessica," she said as she took off her apron.

Nerd Boy inhaled three huge rolls. He barely paused between bites. "You can bring that to my room. Come on."

I swallowed the last bit of my hot chocolate, grabbed a napkin and what was left of my roll, and chased after him.

I wondered how Nerd Boy ate so much and stayed so skinny.

"You wanna look at my baseball cards?" he asked when he shut the door.

Did I!

"I'd love to but—really I thought, well, maybe we could . . . study together."

"Study?!" he said as if I had just asked him to parachute off the top of the house. Nerd Boy probably never had to study.

"Well, yeah, you see I'm having problems with . . . I

thought since . . . You might be able to help me with my math homework."

"Me? Help you?"

"Well, yeah, I know you take all those special classes and all, but . . ."

"So how did you think I would be able to help you?" Nerd Boy glared at me from behind his glasses.

"I . . . I'm . . . having trouble with fractions, and I thought if you explained them to me, I might be able to understand them better."

Nerd Boy didn't answer. He scratched his head.

"Fractions?" he asked, like it was a foreign word.

I swallowed hard. With all the special classes he was taking, he was probably studying logarithms or calculus. Fractions probably sounded like baby stuff to him.

"I know it probably sounds easy to you, being in the gifted class and all, but if you could just help me out . . . I'm desperate."

"Gifted class? What makes you think I'm in gifted classes?"

"Well, you said you took all those special tests and you are in special classes."

Nerd Boy plopped straight down on the floor. His head fell forward and he started shaking. For a second, I thought he was having convulsions. We saw a movie about it in health class once. I was ready to call his mother when he raised his head. He wasn't having convulsions; he was laughing. There wasn't a sound coming from his mouth at first. And then, he started snorting.

"SPECIAL ED" was all he said when he caught his breath. "The special classes are *special education* classes."

It was the first time I had ever seen Nerd Boy smile.

Chapter 15

"Where have you been?" Mom growled.

"I stayed after school for peer tutoring. Math," I stammered.

"Then explain why I just spent the last half hour in front of the school waiting for you."

Stephanie clomped around the corner. She had on her old pair of glasses. Sometimes she wore them when she was pretending to be a teacher. They had big tortoiseshell frames that slid down her nose. She pushed up at them. She sat down at the kitchen table and pretended to read a book. She looked amazingly like Mom as she flipped through the pages and pushed up at her glasses as if she knew what was on each page.

"Michael! Answer me!"

Stephanie froze as if she felt the tension in the air. She dropped her arms to her sides.

"I . . . I stayed after school for tutoring. You can call Ms. Rothchild and ask."

"Michael. It's pouring out. Where have you been?"

"I stopped at Chortle's house."

"How was I to know that! What do you think I am—a mind reader?"

I glanced at the clock thinking it must be nearly six for Mom to be so freaked out. It was five till five. The rule is be home by five.

"It's five to five, Mom."

"It's pouring out. I didn't want you walking in this rain. I waited in front of the school for half an hour. I had no idea where you were."

I just stood there unsure how I should answer. I looked at Stephanie. She still hadn't moved. She was frozen to the chair. It was as if she knew Mom was mad. I can't remember the last time Mom screamed at Stephanie. I can't remember Mom *ever* screaming at Stephanie.

"Answer me! Michael!" Mom's sharp words made me jump. I'm not sure, but I think Stephanie jumped, too.

"It's five to five," I tried again. "I'm supposed to be home at five. I'm not late, Mom. I'm early."

"But it's raining. Pouring. Look at you! You are soaking wet. You'll probably catch pneumonia!"

I wasn't dripping anymore, but my hair was still wet.

"I waited at the school for half an hour," she said again.

"How was I supposed to know you were going to pick me up at school? What am I, *a mind reader*?" I asked.

She didn't answer. Her eyes had the strangest look. We stood there for the longest time. I was afraid to move. Finally, tears came to her eyes and she rushed out of the kitchen and down the hall. I heard her shut her bedroom door.

After she left the kitchen, Stephanie came back to life. She shuffled across the room. She brushed past me, then stopped and felt my arm. "Michael wet. Mom worried," she signed to me, then shuffled off to the refrigerator, opened it, and felt for a can of pop.

In my room, I peeled my wet clothes off and put on my sweat suit. It felt good to be dry again. I plopped on my bed and opened my math book. It might as well have been written in Greek or Swahili. I didn't get it. I rolled on my back. Tomorrow's homework assignment would be another fat zero. The test was just days away. I had walked out on Rothchild's peer tutoring. If Mom did call Ms. Rothchild, I would be in even more trouble. The orthodontist story! I just remembered. Why had I suggested Mom call Ms. Rothchild? She was probably calling her right now. Oh, God! Not only was I flunking math, but I wouldn't be able to play baseball this season and I would probably be grounded for the rest of my life.

The thought was exhausting.

Next thing I knew, Ricky was shaking me awake.

"Mic! Dinner!"

My mouth was dry and my hair was sticking up. It was dark outside. Dad was sitting at the table. I had been so zonked out that I hadn't even heard him come home. Mom didn't seem mad anymore. She was very quiet.

After dinner I knocked softly on the door to Dad's study. He was bent over an engineering journal. He looked up at me. I couldn't see his eyes through the reflection in his glasses. He motioned for me to come in.

"Dad, I need help with math," I said.

With a surprised look, he shut the journal he was reading and motioned for me to sit down.

I never asked Dad to help me with my homework, especially math. He always looked at me like I was stupid and said the answer was right in front of me, but . . . I was desperate.

I shoved the book in front of him. "Problems one through thirty-four—odd," I said. He looked them over and nodded.

"I guess that really means one through thirty-three," he said with a little chuckle.

That was Dad's idea of a major joke. I tried to smile.

He looked over the page, nodding to himself. "OK," he said. He looked at me expectantly.

"I don't know how to do them," I said.

"You are multiplying, dividing, adding, and subtracting."

I knew that. I just didn't know *how* to do it. I didn't say anything. I waited.

"When multiplying, eliminate common factors in the numerator and denominator of the product. Then, multiply the numerators and denominators. When dividing, invert the divisor to change to multiplication. Cancel common factors then multiply the remaining numerators and denominators. OK?"

I shrugged. All I understood in that sentence was *OK*.

He said it so simply, like he was explaining to me how to tie my shoes. Big loop. Little loop. Cross over and pull. Mom had repeated that saying over and over when I was little, but the loops just seemed to fall apart in my hand. I couldn't understand why she just didn't buy Velcro shoes for me. Instead of practicing, I would sneak off to Stephanie's room and ask her to tie my shoes. She always did it very quickly.

"Shhh! Don't tell Mom!" she would sign, then pat me on the head.

I was never sure how she knew Mom wanted me to tie my shoes myself.

"And of course you understand addition and subtraction. With that, all you need to do is use the least common multiple of the denominators as a new denominator or LCD—"

"LCD?"

"Least common denominator. Then add the numerators and change to a mixed number."

I stared at Dad.

"Got it?" Dad asked as he lit his pipe.

"Not really."

"Which part don't you understand?"

"About three-quarters of it," I said. It was my attempt to make a joke.

"Well, which quarter do you understand?"

"Never mind."

He flipped back to the examples in the book. "It's right in front of you."

That was it. The ending statement. Dad wouldn't be able to explain it any better than that.

"Thanks, Dad," I said.

"Anytime." He puffed on his pipe and gave me a smile. As soon as I got up, he went back to reading his journal.

I was doomed. I tossed my math book on the floor next to my backpack and plopped on my bed. When I shut my eyes, the only image that came to mind was Nerd Boy's grin. I could see him on his bedroom floor shaking with silent laughter. The thought made me shudder.

Chapter 16

At lunch Nerd Boy plopped his newspaper carrier's bag down, hit the bench, and shoveled food in. He didn't say anything until he was on the dessert.

I found it hard to eat while he was eating. Every time I looked at him, I remembered how he looked when he smiled. It reminded me of something, but I couldn't quite put my finger on it. I remembered as he scraped the last bit of apple pie from the corners of his tray, the Cheshire cat in Ricky's *Alice in Wonderland* book. A Cheshire cat with a big nose and glasses.

I worried for a second that he might mention math or fractions in front of the guys. Somehow I knew he wouldn't. I think he knew it would embarrass me.

The minute the spoon came out of his mouth, he was on his feet. He didn't even wait for his watch alarm today. "Later, Four-Twelve." He gathered up his things and was gone. He usually only spent half of his lunch period at our table. I wondered what he did for the rest of the lunch period.

"Stolksie," Freemont snorted. "I think we've just been snubbed."

Stolks scratched his head.

"Tell me, *Four-Twelve*, have you two sweet boys been having secret sock meetings?"

That's right. I'd been to Nerd Boy's room twice now and I hadn't seen his socks.

"I forgot again," I said without thinking.

"Forgot again? *You went there again?!*"

I turned red. "Well, I . . ." You always had to think around Freemont.

"Don't give me any of this baseball stuff again. It was raining yesterday. Or maybe Sock Boy has special waterproof socks that protected you from the rain? That's it, isn't it! Do you have yours on now?" He peeked under the table.

"Careful," I said. "I could be wearing my 007 socks." Sometimes the best way to handle Freemont is to play along.

"Mic wanted me to tell you that you look lovely today," Freemont said to Julia Patterson as we left our last hour class.

I punched him in the upper arm. He tried to punch me back, but I jumped out of his way. He chased me all the way back to my locker. When I stopped, he caught me and punched me back.

"I ran all the way for that? I hardly felt it," I lied. I could feel the indentation of each of his knuckles throbbing on my arm.

He wound up to hit me again. I sunk to the floor, still panting from the chase. Freemont let his fist drop and sunk down on the floor next to me.

Stolks shuffled up to us. He shoved a whole half of a Mounds bar into his mouth. "Where'd you guys go in such a hurry?" he asked through a mouthful of chocolate and coconut.

I opened my locker and dumped my load of books inside with a thud that reverberated off the door. Just then Godzilla Girl waddled up. "Get your door out of my way," she grumbled.

I ignored her.

"Hey, let's go to Mic's house and watch his sister run into walls," Freemont said, slapping me hard on the back.

"Move it," Godzilla Girl growled, shoving my locker door shut.

"Forget it, Freemont," I said. I clicked my lock in place and brushed past Freemont and Stolks. "Mom has Girl Scouts at our house this afternoon."

"Oh, a real freak show," he said, and grinned.

"Sort of." I shrugged.

When I was about two blocks from home, Nerd Boy came up to me on his bike. "Sorry I laughed yesterday."

The picture of Vern shaking with silent laughter would probably stay with me for the rest of my life.

"I wasn't laughing at you," he said.

"Whatever," I mumbled.

"I mean, I know how it is not to understand school stuff. Especially numbers," he said as he got off his bike and started to walk beside me. "Dyscalculia," he said.

"Dis . . . what?" I asked.

"Dyscalculia. It's a math learning disability."

"Never heard of it," I said. It sounded like a disease involving Count Dracula.

"I've got it. Been in special classes since I was in first grade," he said. "I turn numbers around. It's not just school stuff. It makes it hard for me to remember people's names and keep track of time and remember the layout of things and use money."

I looked at him funny.

"If numbers give you problems, then why do you call me Four-Twelve?"

"I learned the number of your house before I learned

your name. Once in a while a number sticks in my mind. Four-Twelve stuck."

We walked awhile not saying anything.

"Sorry," I finally said. "I mean . . . I didn't know."

"The worst part is I don't remember scores of games, and it's hard for me to keep up with the count when I'm pitching."

"That must really be tough."

"Yeah, so I didn't mean to laugh," he said. "It's just that no one ever thought I was smart before. Why did you?"

I shrugged. What could I say—I thought he was a nerd and that all nerds were smart?

"Anyway, sorry I laughed. It seemed important to you."

"It is. If I don't learn fractions and pull up my grade, I can't play baseball."

Nerd Boy stopped dead in his tracks. I walked past him a few steps before I realized. I turned back to him. His mouth was hanging open in shock. It looked like the last breath had been sucked out of him.

"No baseball," he gasped.

I nodded.

"This is serious."

"I know," I said.

Nerd Boy stood there like a zombie. Suddenly, he came to life, jumped on his bike, and pedaled off with lightning speed.

Mom was just pulling into the driveway when I got home. She scrambled out of the car dangling bags from each arm. She struggled with the door, then pushed her way in. Stephanie got out of the car and walked past as Mom struggled to keep a carton of eggs from slipping out of a bag.

"I'm going to need your help, Michael," she said as she

stepped around Stephanie on her way back to the car for the second load. Ricky had just climbed into the front seat and pretended he was driving.

So what else is new? I thought as I sank to the backdoor steps and waited for instructions.

"First, get Ricky settled in your room. We're making pretzels for the cooking badge. Could you get the ingredients out for me? I left the list on the counter." She grunted as she hauled another load into the house. She didn't even wait for me to answer.

"Come on, Ricky." I tugged at his T-shirt.

"I'm driving." He grinned up at me.

"Well, drive into my room," I said.

He stuck out his lower lip.

"I'll give you a piggyback ride," I offered as a bribe.

"Peanuts, too?" he asked.

I nodded. "Yup."

"Deal," he said, giving me a low five and then a high five.

I galloped with Ricky and Peanuts into the house, around the living room two times, and down the hall to my bedroom. I guess Stephanie could feel the house shake as I galloped, because she stopped, held out her hand, and laughed. I dumped Ricky on my bed and ran to get the portable TV out of Mom and Dad's bedroom. I switched on *Sesame Street.*

Next, I went to the kitchen to get the ingredients out for today's romp in the kitchen. Just as I started, the doorbell rang. Soon the living room was full of deaf Girl Scouts with loud nasal voices and flailing arms as they signed to each other. Stephanie stood in the middle of the room rebounding off everyone like a ball in a pinball machine.

"Hurry and finish," Mom called as she flashed by with another load of things.

A couple of other deaf girls came into the kitchen while I was working. Linda's about my age, but a whole head taller. She looked at me out of the corner of her eye and signed wildly to the cluster of girls around her. Bangle bracelets slid up and down her arm, clinking and clanking as her hands jerked about. She only mouthed the words, popping her lips together and making a smacking sound.

My signing is not that good; I know she said *brother* and *boy* and *cute* and something that looked like *past* or *late*. I wish I could remember more. Whatever it was, it made the group of them laugh. They kept looking at me, then looking away and laughing. I pretended I didn't notice them, but my cheeks were red-hot and the tops of my ears were burning.

Someone's hearing aid was feeding back. The squeak and squeal pierced my ears. Mom didn't seem to notice. I was ready to go out of my mind. I couldn't tell whose hearing aid it was coming from. I bet the CIA uses the same frequency to break enemy agents.

"Mom," I called over their heads. "Someone's hearing aid . . ."

Mom seemed to notice the noise for the first time. She looked around and tapped a girl with pigtails and motioned for her to turn down her hearing aid.

The doorbell rang and Mrs. Peters came in with Deanie. I hadn't seen Deanie since last summer. She went away to a residential school for the deaf and blind in Boston last fall. She looked exactly the same.

She has short, fluffy white-blond hair and big blue glasses with thick Coke-bottle lenses that magnify her big, blank, blue eyes. She always wears white kneesocks.

Her mother had one arm around her as she led her through the door. Deanie's mom sat Deanie down gently and took her coat off for her. Deanie looked like a limp rag doll. Mrs. Peters smoothed her hair, pulled up Deanie's kneesocks, and folded her hands in her lap. Sitting there with her perfect hair and perfect white socks, Deanie looked perfectly normal.

Deanie sat motionless for a second, staring blankly at the floor. Then, an unseen rhythm took her body and rocked it ever so slowly back and forth, till her mother noticed and put a hand out to stop her.

Mom worked her way to Deanie and fingerspelled something in her hand. A small, rare smile crept to Deanie's face.

Mom used to be Deanie's teacher. She tried to do things with Deanie outside school, too. Mom said the toughest part of teaching Deanie was dealing with Deanie's mother.

Meanwhile, Linda brought Stephanie into the living room. Stephanie was so happy, she was beaming. Her hair frizzed wildly around her face. She had a big red goose egg glowing in the middle of her forehead. She'd run into something again. Stephanie rubbed the bump softly.

"Ow-w-w-w-w-w," she howled, still smiling. She put one hand on Linda's throat to see if she was laughing.

With my part in this disaster finished, I pushed my way through the crowd of whistling hearing aids, screeches, and wheeling arms to the safety of my room. I shut the door and put the desk chair in front of it, just in case.

Chapter 17

I came out only when I heard the front door close for the last time. Sometime in the middle of the Girl Scout meeting, Dad came home from work and retreated to his study. I wonder if he put a chair in front of his door.

The kitchen was in shambles. There was flour everywhere. Where it didn't dust the counter or the floor, there were floury footprints and handprints. Mom was gone but soon returned with two bags from McDonald's.

"I want a Happy Meal," Ricky whined.

"We all have the same thing," Mom said in her teacher's voice.

Stephanie had already grabbed a handful of fries and was cramming them into her mouth.

"But I want a Happy Meal," Ricky whined.

"Ricky, do you want a strawberry or a chocolate shake?" Mom asked, trying to distract him.

Meanwhile, Stephanie was sampling all the shakes.

"Mom," I cried.

Mom signed "no" to her and gently pulled her hand away. Stephanie hooted and grabbed at the tray of shakes, knocking two to the floor. One of the tops popped open on impact, and strawberry shake oozed out over the flour-dusted floor. Mom took Stephanie out of the room to clean the shake from her shoes. Dad said nothing. He shook his head and started cleaning up the spilled shake.

Mom looked tired when she came back to the table. Especially her eyes. They had big bags under them.

We ate in silence.

Then Mom said, "I've been thinking. A Seeing Eye dog would help Stephanie get around. She could use the companionship."

A dog, I thought. *I've always wanted a dog.*

Mom continued to talk about the Seeing Eye dog program. Dad ate his burger like he wasn't listening, but I knew he was. I also knew by the way he blinked his eyes that he didn't like the idea.

I looked at the kitchen. Mom had cleared a spot on the table for us to eat. I thought of Chortle's immaculate kitchen, the hot chocolate with the glob of whipped cream plopped expertly on top and the smell of homemade fresh-baked cinnamon rolls.

"I wish I could have homemade cinnamon rolls for dessert," I blurted out.

Mom couldn't have looked more surprised if I had asked for a pet elephant.

"What?" she asked.

"Homemade cinnamon rolls," I said, a little embarrassed. "Vern's mother makes homemade cinnamon rolls every week."

Stephanie knocked something over in her room. There was a loud crash followed by stamping and hooting.

Mom pushed away from the table, glaring at me as if I had caused the problem down the hall.

Dad must have been pretty tired, because he didn't take the opportunity to yell at me. He just lifted his glasses, rubbed his eyes, and gave his head a shake as if to shake away bad thoughts.

Later that night, I heard my parents arguing again.

"Maggie, I just don't think it's a good idea."

"Why not?"

I tiptoed to the door, cracked it open slightly, crouched down, and listened.

"Well, I don't think the benefits outweigh the expense," Dad said.

"I'm not talking about buying a mink coat or a pool table. This is an item pertinent to your daughter's development."

"But a dog requires a lot of maintenance. And a Seeing Eye dog is expensive," Dad countered.

"I say we forget about how expensive it is and just do it," Mom interrupted. "We'll worry about how to pay for it later."

"Forget about how expensive it is?" Dad asked. "But what happens when . . ."

"What happens when! What happens when what?" Mom screamed at him. "You mean: What happens when Stephanie goes away to school!"

"I didn't say that," Dad said.

"You've already given up! How can you turn your back on your daughter. Your only daughter!" She was crying now. "How can you exile her from where she belongs to an . . . an institution?"

"Maggie, it's not an institution. It's a school," Dad said, trying to calm Mom down. "Maggie, you're too emotional about this to be objective."

"How can you be so detached?" she sniffed.

"Maybe it's the best thing for everyone involved," Dad said.

"An institution?" Mom sobbed.

"A school."

Mom continued to yell at Dad. Their voices grew louder

and angrier. I closed the door and crept back to bed.

A fear grabbed my whole body. I put my pillow over my head and tried to block out the loud angry words from across the hall. I squeezed my eyes shut so tightly, they hurt.

She ruins everything, I thought. Now my parents were fighting. Maybe they would get divorced. All because of her.

Chapter 18

Saturday morning I woke to the sound of Mom unloading groceries. She left the pop cans on the kitchen counter. I have to make braille labels to go on the cans so when Stephanie pokes her fingers into the refrigerator, she'll know exactly what she is getting.

I struggled to peel the Mountain Dew sticker away from its backing. When it did, it stuck to my fingers. I shook it off. It flew over the bar, slid across the floor, and disappeared under the refrigerator.

The doorbell rang. I stepped over Ricky, who was lying in front of the TV entranced with *Scooby Doo,* and opened the door.

"Hey, Mic." Freemont grinned. "Ready to hit the arcade?"

"Who is it?" Mom called from the bedroom.

"David," I yelled back. "Come in."

"How about it?" He grinned.

I think he knew the answer would be no and he couldn't wait to rub it in.

Mom came down the hall with an armful of dirty sheets. "Hello, David," she said.

"Hi," he grunted. "Well?" he asked.

Mom was halfway down the basement stairs. "Mom," I called after her. "Can I go to the arcade?"

"Are the labels done?" she called back.

Case closed.

"I have to put labels on Stephanie's drinks," I said. Stephanie wandered into the living room smiling at nothing. She tripped over Ricky, started to gulp-laugh, and reached out to find him. When she did, she tickled him.

"Ow! Stop it," he yelled.

"How many you gotta do?" Freemont asked.

"A dozen or so," I replied over the noise in the living room.

"I'll help," Freemont said. He peeled off his coat as he straddled a chair.

I started punching on the label maker.

"What's that say?" he asked.

"Mountain Dew."

"OK." He grinned and stuck the label on an orange pop can.

"Mountain Dew," I repeated.

He grinned devilishly and chuckled. "I figure if we have to do it, we should make it fun."

Freemont had always known how to make things fun. He was the one who had taught me how to turn my eyelids inside out. At sleepovers, he was the one who came up with the best prank phone calls. In fourth grade, he had started the tradition of stapler wars whenever we had a sub. And despite what all the subs said, no one had put an eye out— though a few of us had spent a couple of hours in detention because of it.

By the time Mom returned from starting the laundry, we were putting the last cans in the refrigerator.

"Finished with the cans?"

I nodded, afraid if I spoke I would start laughing.

"Can I go now?" I managed to say.

She didn't say anything. I could see the wheels turning; she had something else planned for me.

"Can I?" I asked again.

"Be back for lunch at noon."

"By noon?!" Mom's look stopped me. Besides, I had something important to ask. "My allowance?"

She reached around Stephanie for her purse. Ricky raced into the room shouting, "Scooby Dooby Dooo-ooo, where are yoooo-ooou!" He slammed into her legs and put a death lock on her knees. She wavered back and forth as she handed me five dollars.

"Don't spend it all in one place," she said.

I took the money and put my coat on. With a ten-minute walk each way, I'd have less than an hour to spend at the arcade. But with only five dollars, I'd run out of money before I ran out of time.

Stephanie pulled a can of pop from the refrigerator just as we were going out the door. We walked slowly down the driveway. We heard her bellowing from there. She sounded like a wounded cow. We both looked at each other and broke into a run. It was damp out. The smell of wet sidewalks stung my nose. Our feet splattered against the pavement. We ran about a block and had to stop because we were laughing so hard. We dropped to our knees in the front of the Pepto-Bismol house. Droplets clung to the newly green grass and soaked into my knees. We laughed all the way to the arcade.

When I got home, everyone appeared calm. Ricky had his miniature car track set up in the living room. A long line of cars waited for their turn on the track.

"Home just in time," Mom called from the kitchen when she heard the front door shut.

For once, I thought. *At least I did one thing right this week.*

Mom put a platter of grilled cheese sandwiches on the table. She cut them wrong again. Rectangles instead of triangles. She was serving them with chips and the barfo pickles that Aunt Sue makes. No one likes them but Aunt Sue and Mom. I'd put them down the disposal, but I'm afraid they would eat through the pipes.

"Ricky, come eat," Mom called.

"Just one more," Ricky said as he sent the red '56 Chevy with yellow flames on the fenders speeding down the track. He gave it too much of a push and it careened off the track, flipped end to end, and skidded into the kitchen. Ricky made crash noises followed by an ambulance siren. He drove to the chair, climbed up, and sat on his knees.

Mom stomped on the floor to get Stephanie's attention. She moved to her and fingerspelled "lunch" into her hand. Stephanie shuffled two steps to the table. Her foot flew out from under her as she stepped on Ricky's car. She landed on the kitchen floor with a SMACK! A momentary look of surprise crossed her face. She groped across the kitchen floor, searching for what had made her fall. When she found the car, she broke into gulp-laughs.

"Ricky," Mom snapped so sharply it even made me jump. "How many times have I told you not to leave cars lying around. You're lucky Stephanie's not seriously hurt!"

Stephanie tried to tickle Ricky. Poor little guy burst into tears. When Stephanie felt the first teardrop, she stopped cold. Her face went expressionless. Her eyes flickered back into her head and her mouth dropped open. She stood frozen for a moment, then sat down as if nothing had happened.

Ricky rolled up into a little hurt blob and sobbed. Mom started to sign where everything was on Stephanie's plate, but she grunted and pushed Mom's hand away.

We ate in silence except for the constant smacking that goes with all our meals. I watched cheese and bread somersaulting over and over in Stephanie's mouth. I tried to look past her without seeing anything.

"We had problems with the labels you did today," Mom said.

"Really?" I answered. I wondered if that sounded too fake.

"Yes," she said, dabbing at the corners of her mouth with a napkin. "It seems twelve of the eighteen cans were mislabeled."

"Really! Twelve!" I said. I tried to sound surprised. "Sorry. Guess David distracted me."

"I repositioned them. I hope they stay stuck on."

"Oh, I'm sure they will," I said.

"I almost forgot, that kid from down the street . . . What's his name?"

"Ner— Vern?"

I drank down the last drop of milk and pushed away from the table.

"Yes, Vern called and asked if you wanted to go to the batting cages with them this afternoon. You were supposed to call him right away."

"Can I?"

"I guess so."

I leaped out of the chair and pecked out the number Mom had written on the chalkboard next to the phone.

"OK," Vern said. "Can we pick you up in fifteen minutes?"

As soon as my hand left the receiver, I was showered with cold milk. I blinked hard and shook the milk from my eyes and nostrils. Sputtering, I turned around. Stephanie started gulp-laughing and reached out to feel my matted bangs. I wound up to punch her right in that happy smile of hers.

"Michael, no!" Mom shouted, and pulled Stephanie out of my reach. She dragged Stephanie from the room and returned with a towel.

"Go take a shower and wash your hair. I'll start on the kitchen." She sighed as she looked at the milk-splattered walls, floor, and refrigerator.

"But Nerd— Vern's coming . . ."

"Hurry up then," she said. At least she didn't try to make excuses for Stephanie this time.

I knew why this had happened. Stephanie has the memory of an elephant and the vengeance of a pit viper. She has an eerie sense of what is an accident and what is deliberate. This was her way of getting even for the cans.

I clenched my fist and punched her door hard as I passed it on the way to the bathroom. I wished I could put my fist right through it. Instead, my knuckles turned bright red. They were still throbbing when I turned off the shower.

I heard Mom talking to Vern in the foyer. I ran to my room, threw on a pair of jeans and a sweatshirt, and pulled my baseball cap over my wet hair.

"Sorry," I said as the storm door slammed. I kicked the newspaper from the porch. I wished I could have sent it into orbit, but it only ricocheted off the hedge with a dull thud.

Vern shrugged. "No problem," he said.

Chapter 19

Why hadn't I ever had a coach like Mr. Chortle? After just thirty minutes in the batting cage with him coaching me, I felt I could hit anything. From anyone! Even left-handed Vernon Chortle. If only I had a new glove, then I'd be able to catch anything.

Of course, I've never had a baseball coach sing to me. About five minutes after I got there, I smacked one way out there and Mr. Chortle started singing and waving his arms around. "BRAVO! Bell-meecy-something," he would sing whenever I hit one far. I nearly jumped out of my skin the first time he did that. I looked at Vern. He didn't seemed surprised or startled or embarrassed—even though everyone was staring at us. Maybe he's into that opera stuff, too.

When we got back to the car, Mr. Chortle turned to Vern and asked, "What do you think, Vern? It's warm enough today, isn't it?"

Vern shrugged as if he didn't care one way or the other.

"OK, boys. Get ready for some wind in your hair," Mr. Chortle said. He pushed a button on the dashboard and the convertible top lifted and folded slowly back behind me.

"You know what this means," Mr. Chortle said.

"Yeah. Yeah." Vern nodded as if this happened every day.

"Ice cream. You can't ride in a convertible the first time

without an ice-cream cone. It's a tradition. Point the way to the closest spot, Mic?"

"Turn right at the corner," I said as he cranked up the stereo. The speakers hummed and vibrated with a deep male voice. Mr. Chortle sang along. I had noticed at the batting cages he couldn't sing without waving his arms around. At least while he was driving he kept one hand on the steering wheel.

"A *glorióso* day, no?," he asked in his best Italian accent.

I nodded and shrunk lower in the seat. Luckily, he turned down the stereo as we went through the drive-thru at McDonald's. I hoped someone would see me in the back of this cool convertible—but not notice who I was with or the opera yowling on the stereo.

"Wanna see some videotapes of the championship series last year, Mic?" Mr. Chortle asked as we left the drive-thru.

I nodded.

The Chortle house smelled great. Mrs. Chortle had been baking again. This time she had made fat, gooey brownies cut in perfectly square pieces with half a walnut perfectly centered on top just like on the box. They were great!

We sat in front of their big-screen TV as Mr. Chortle told me about their championship year.

Vern didn't say a word as Mr. Chortle described the whole season game after game, highlighting the odd or fantastic plays through the playoffs all the way to the state championships. The way he described it to me, I felt like I had been there.

"Is the Pony League strong here?" he asked.

"It's OK. Not state championship material." I looked across the table at Nerd Boy. Vern was tipped back in his chair and staring at the ceiling. "At least not last year."

"First things first." Mr. Chortle stood and stretched.

"First we've got to make the team. Right, boys?" He slapped us both on the back and walked into the kitchen.

"Got that math thing worked out yet?" Vern asked after his father left the room.

I shook my head no.

"Come with me."

I followed him upstairs.

"Wait in there," he said, pointing to his room.

I sat in his desk chair.

"Jessica does well in math," he said as he left the room.

He walked down the hall and tapped softly on his sister's door. There was no answer. I knew she was in there; we had heard her talking on the phone when we had passed by the room. He tapped again, a little louder this time. When there still was no answer, he opened the door and went in.

"What do you want?" she screeched.

I couldn't hear what Vern asked. Jessica's response could be heard down the block.

"Yeah, right! As if moving to this crappy town wasn't traumatic enough, now my geek brother wants me to tutor his geek friends. Get out! *Get out!*"

I don't know what bothered me most—knowing she thought my hometown was crappy or realizing she thought I was as geeky as Vern.

"She's sixteen," a voice said from somewhere in the room.

I jumped a foot. My heart leaped into my throat.

Angela's head popped out from under the bed. "Mom says if we just ignore her, she'll grow out of most of this stuff." She held her finger to her lips signaling me to be quiet and disappeared under the bed. The bedspread fell back in place as Vern came in the room.

"It was worth a try." He shrugged and sat on the bed directly over where Angela had disappeared.

Silently, Angela's hand appeared from under the bed-spread and inched closer to Vern's ankle.

Vern pulled his sweatshirt over his head and tossed it toward his closet. At the same time he swung his legs out of reach. "Touch the socks and you die," he said.

She pounded the floor.

"Someday," she said as she scrambled out from under the bed and stomped from the room.

"Never," he called down the hall after her. He shut the door.

"The most precious pair of socks in my collection."

"Really?" I asked.

They were the most ordinary socks I had seen on him. They looked like any old pair of athletic socks to me.

"Not much to look at, are they?" he said as he carefully removed them.

"Not really."

"They once belonged to Nolan Ryan."

"Really? Where'd you get them?"

"Celebrity auction," he said.

"Uh, Vern? Why do you have all these maps on the back of your bedroom door?" I asked.

"The dyscalculia makes it hard for me to find places."

I thought of the laminated map of the school he still carried around with him.

"You are here?" I asked.

"Exactly. And time is another problem. I used to be late for class all the time. That's why my parents gave me a programmable watch," he said. He hit the button on it so it would go off—like I hadn't heard it before.

"I'm going to hand-wash my socks and take a shower," he said. He opened the bedroom door. "You can spend the night if you'd like," he called back over his shoulder.

Chapter 20

I almost left the house while he was in the shower. I don't know if it would have mattered either way to Vern.

He didn't act surprised or glad that I was still there after his shower. He just nodded when I asked if I could call my mom.

Mr. Chortle ordered pizza for dinner.

Jessica grabbed a slice and ran upstairs.

"Isn't Jessica going to eat with us?" I asked.

"She thinks she's too good for us," Angela said.

"Wait until you're sixteen," said Mrs. Chortle. "All sixteen-year-old girls are like that."

Stephanie would be sixteen on her next birthday.

Halfway through the pizza, Mrs. Chortle started asking me about the neighborhood.

I described all the weird sites along Bixby Court: Mr. Petrowski and his webbed fingers at 422, Mrs. Marston and the ghost of Houdini at 418. The Pepto-Bismol house had already caught their attention, as well as Sam, the three-legged golden retriever. I told them how Sam had lost his right front leg. I never told them about my weird family. I wondered if Vern had told them?

We played Sega World Series Baseball most of the night. I was dying to see Vern's sock collection but didn't ask.

I couldn't wait to see what he would sleep in. Did he have

special sleepy-time socks? I was disappointed. He slept in a plain old white T-shirt and pair of boxer shorts. He was sockless. Without his glasses, he looked like a mole with no eyes at all.

"Get that math thing worked out, Four-Twelve," he said from his bed when I was getting ready to leave the next morning. "You got to. You're the only person I know who's trying out for the team." He rolled over and started snoring—just the way he had most of the night.

I rolled up the sleeping bag and tiptoed from the house.

Spending the night with Nerd Boy did not get me out of going to church. I raced home at 10:40 and changed. We missed the opening hymn, but it wasn't my fault. They didn't have to wait for me.

Julia Patterson was sitting at the end of our pew. She waved when we first arrived. Did she really think I'd wave back? I could feel her staring at me through the whole service.

Gramps's big ol' blue Pontiac was in front of the house when we got home from church.

Grammy died two years ago. I still miss her. She was a Cardinals fan. If she had come today, she would have brought me new baseball cards and we could have talked about Ozzie Smith and some old-timer named Stan Musial.

Gramps is another story. He is a big guy with a clump of white hair on the top of his head and curly white chest hair that pours out of the top of his V-neck T-shirt. He looks mad all the time and tells boring navy stories.

He has a key to the house but always waits for us in the car. He waited until we got out of our car and into the house before he slowly got out of the Pontiac and lumbered to the door.

He rang the doorbell like we didn't notice him in his car in front of the house.

"Pop." Mom smiled and gave her dad a big hug.

"Where's my little Stephanie?" he bellowed as he hugged Mom.

"She's very excited about seeing you," Mom said. "Ricky, go get your sister."

Ricky ran down the hall. Seconds later Stephanie clomped down the hall. Her eyes flitted back in her head. Her smile was ear to ear. She gave Gramps a big hug and hooted.

"Tell her I got a surprise for her," Gramps said to Mom. Gramps is the only person who gets away with not signing to Stephanie. Mom refuses to interpret for anyone in the family. Even Ricky has to talk to Stephanie himself, not through Mom. Sometimes Mom forms the letters in Ricky's hand and places his hand in Stephanie's, but she would never talk *for* Ricky.

Grammy was pretty good at fingerspelling. She often relayed Gramps's words to Stephanie's hand.

I used to interpret for Stephanie at big family gatherings. Grown-ups gossip over kids' heads all the time. They think we don't hear or understand what they are talking about. Stephanie would laugh aloud at what they said. My aunts and uncles had no idea that I was relaying their conversation from my hand to her hand under the table.

As I watched Ricky spell something in Stephanie's hand, I tried to remember the last time I had said *anything* to Stephanie. I couldn't. I felt a sudden pang of guilt.

Gramps's surprise for Stephanie was a string. Stephanie followed the string out the front door, down the porch steps, and around the side of the house.

Hidden behind a big juniper bush was a shiny silver tandem bike. Stephanie felt the handlebars and the front wheel. Then she ran her hand over the seat and across the second set of handlebars. Stephanie started hooting. She felt the second seat and the first seat over and over. She felt the two handlebars, then climbed on the first seat and grinned. Gramps let out a monstrous laugh.

"Now we can ride bikes as a family!" Mom smiled.

The idea of Dad pedaling around on his old black clunker made me laugh.

"And Stephanie could use the exercise," Mom said softly, as if Stephanie might hear her and be offended.

I wondered who was going to get roped into pedaling her around all summer. If they thought they were going to get me on a bike for a mobile freak show, they better think again.

Ricky pulled at my leg. "Do you think Gramps brought a present for me?"

Fat chance, I thought. I picked Ricky up and swung him around. Poor kid. He was too little to know that only disabled grandchildren got presents. I learned that a long time ago.

Gramps inspected the tandem one more time before anyone got on it again. He checked each nut and bolt, "stem to stern," as he loved to say. He tightened the nut on the second set of handlebars.

When Mom went into the house to get the video camera, Gramps inspected Ricky.

"Come here, boy," he bellowed.

Ricky ran over.

"What's two plus one?" Gramps quizzed.

Ricky's eyes went up as he concentrated. He counted on his fingers behind his back. "Three!" Ricky shouted.

"Do you know your ABC's?" Gramps drilled.

Ricky nodded and started in a singsongy voice, "A, B, C, D . . ." all the way to Z.

"Let me see you tie your shoe," Gramps commanded.

Ricky fumbled around with his shoelaces and only managed to twist them up in a ball.

"Gotta work on that, don't you?" Gramps shook his head seriously. Gramps never gave up until he found something you couldn't do, then he would tell you to work on it.

Dad climbed on the front and steadied the bike for Stephanie. Mom videotaped their maiden bike trip down to the end of the street and back. Ricky ran along the side.

I was left alone with Gramps.

"Come over here, boy. Tell me about school," he said.

"It's OK." I shrugged.

"How are your grades?" he demanded.

"OK," I repeated.

"OK?" he said, shaking his head with a scowl. "Got to do better than OK to get by in this world. Got to study, boy. College diplomas don't grow on trees." He took a deep breath and sat back.

Dad had turned the mobile freak show around and was pedaling back toward the house. Ricky had run the entire length of the block. He was only four, and even though there were two of them pedaling, Ricky was keeping up with them. He was fast.

"Michael," Gramps said, pounding his fist into his other hand. "You can't sit back and expect things to be given to you on a silver platter. You've got to *earn* your way in this world."

I watched Mom help Stephanie from the bike. Stephanie was beaming. *Wanna bet,* I thought.

"I don't know about kids today. They always have those things in their ears, blasting their brains out with that darn music. When I was a kid not much older than you, I went into the navy . . ."

Oh boy, I thought. *Here we go again.* There was no stopping him now. I peeked at my watch to see how long this lecture would last. I wished I had my Walkman to drone out his noise.

Chapter 21

After Gramps left, I went to my room to study fractions. The test was tomorrow. It was hopeless. I wasn't any closer to understanding how to multiply, divide, add, or subtract fractions than I was a week ago.

Stephanie shuffled into the room. Mom had washed her hair. Even when it was wet, her hair curled, frizzed, and sprang wildly around her face. She sat down on the edge of the bed where I was sprawled out with all of my books and stared blankly across the room as if she was waiting for me to do something.

I wasn't in the mood to talk to anyone.

"Mic worried," she signed. "What for?"

I blinked hard. How did she know I was worried?

"Mic worried," she signed again. "What for?" She placed her right hand on my shoulder.

I shrugged.

With her left hand she felt the books and papers on the bed.

"What subject?" she signed.

"M-A-T-H," I spelled into her hand.

"Problem? Worry?" she signed back to me.

"F-R-A-C-T-I-O-N-S," I spelled in her hand.

She stared past me for a long time, then stood and shuffled from the room.

She returned five minutes later, carrying a big shoe box. She had her slate and stylus, a spiral notebook, and her brailler. For some reason she put on her old pair of glasses. Her eyes looked huge and empty behind the thick lenses. She sat down on the floor and spread the materials around her.

"MY-Y-Y-Y-Y-Y," she hooted and then silently signed. "Mic, come. I teach."

I was so desperate, I didn't even think about protesting. I sat down on the floor with her.

"Addition. Write problem," she signed, and pushed the notebook and stylus to me.

It had been a long time since I had written with the braille pencil, called a stylus. I turned the notebook page and wrote the problem backward from right to left. When I was finished, I turned the page back to the front and put it on Stephanie's lap.

Stephanie felt the problem and nodded. She took the lid from the shoe box and felt around until she found the circles she wanted. She put two circles in front of me that were divided into parts, like fractions. She wrote on the notebook the rule for addition. Stephanie set up the problem with the plastic fraction pieces.

Gently she took my hand and led it over the braille page. Then she put the circles in my hand. She changed the $\frac{2}{3}$ into $\frac{4}{6}$.

"Same," she signed.

She changed the $\frac{1}{2}$ into $\frac{3}{6}$.

"Same," she signed again.

She put the two together.

"Answer?" she asked.

"$1\frac{1}{6}$," I wrote with the stylus on the page.

"Right!" Her face lit up and her big blue eyes flitted back into her head.

Slowly and patiently, she worked me through addition, subtraction, multiplication, and division.

I had seen the same rules on the board many times. I had read them in my math book. I had heard the same words come from Ms. Rothchild's mouth over and over again. But now for the first time, I was feeling the rules for addition, subtraction, multiplication, and division through my fingers. It was as if the tips of my fingers were absorbing the information from the raised letters on the page and transferring it to my brain.

I kept making mistakes, but Stephanie patiently corrected me. Not once did she make me feel stupid. As I felt the rules and felt the problems come to life under my fingers piece by piece, I suddenly understood. What had been abstract mumbo jumbo now made sense.

When I answered ten problems correctly without having to use the plastic circles, Stephanie put all the circles back together and put them in the shoe box. She gathered the notebook, slate and stylus, and brailler and stood. She took off her glasses. Her eyes seemed just as large and blank without the Coke-bottle lenses to magnify them. She folded her glasses and placed them on the pile in front of her.

"Mic understand. Mic no worry now. Good night," she signed, and shuffled from the room.

I dreamed about fractions all night.

Chapter 22

I placed the test on Ms. Rothchild's desk.

"When will these be graded?" I asked.

"I'll have them back to you by Thursday."

"THURSDAY!"

"I have six classes, Mic. That's over two hundred tests to grade," Ms. Rothchild replied.

"Maybe just this one time you could grade this one first and let me know right away."

Ms. Rothchild looked at me funny. I didn't know if she was laughing at me behind those glasses or getting mad. "Hurry, Mic, or you'll be late for your next class."

I had been the last one in the class to turn in my test, but it wasn't because I was the last to finish. I had finished with ten minutes to spare and had taken that time to recheck all my work.

It was as if some magic door had been opened. I understood all the squiggles on the paper. I understood! It wasn't foreign or complicated. Once I understood the four rules, it was easy. Unbelievably easy.

I was certain I had aced the test. I checked every problem carefully to make sure that I hadn't made any stupid little mistakes. I had even tried to write neatly.

Pony League sign-up ended Friday. I needed this grade

to convince Mom to let me sign up. My life was on hold until I got the test back.

When Ms. Rothchild didn't return the test Friday morning, I thought I would burst. After class I pleaded my case.

"I'll have them Monday. I promise, Mic," Ms. Rothchild said as she shuffled papers on her desk.

"I need to know today!"

"Mic, the bell is going to ring in the next three minutes; I have another class and I'm not writing you a pass."

"My last three quizzes were F's. My mom had to write how she felt about that on the back of each quiz. I've been in the doghouse for weeks."

"Mic, I have another class."

"PLEEEEEEASE." I got down on one knee.

I've never seen Ms. Rothchild blush, but the red that crept up her neck and took over her face was way beyond a blush. She turned beet red. "Mic. Stand up. I think I have yours graded. Just this once." She flipped through the file of tests from first hour until she found my test. She showed me the grade at the top.

I hadn't aced it. A minus. I was almost disappointed. *Great Job!* was written across the top.

"Now get to class," Ms. Rothchild said trying to sound stern, but I could see a little smile on her lips. "NOW!"

I wanted to see which problems I had missed, but I knew that was out of the question. I was out the door and down the hall when it hit me—the test score would raise my grade from a D to at least a B minus, perhaps even a B. "YESSSS!" I shouted. Several teachers scowled at me.

"Walk!" Mr. Burgess reminded me.

I could have flown to my next class.

Chapter 23

"Vern," I said as soon as the newspaper carrier's bag hit the floor on the other side of the lunchroom table. "Guess what!"

Vern barely sat down before he started shoveling in the special of the day. He didn't say anything.

"I passed! I got an A minus. That means I'll get a B minus, maybe even a B. I can sign up for tryouts!"

"Great," he said through a mouthful of green beans.

"An A minus! An A minus! An A minus! I can't believe it!"

"Stolksie baby, I think we are interrupting a Kodak moment. These two were about to hug and kiss," Fremont said.

"Yeah, right." I tried to laugh. I could feel sweat breaking out on my forehead.

"Say, VERNON, do you have special tryout socks you wear just for Pony League baseball?"

I was afraid Vern would tell him about his Nolan Ryan socks, but Vern kept shoveling in green beans and didn't say a word.

"Come on, VERNON, you can tell *me* all about it. Are you wearing them now?"

Suddenly, I thought Vern might think I had told Freemont about the socks. I shook my head at the thought.

Freemont reached under the table and pulled at Vern's

pant legs. Vern pulled away from him. Finished with his green beans, he attacked the chocolate pudding.

"Cut it out, Freemont," I said. "Leave him alone."

"OOOOH, I'm scared. You sock boys really stick together."

Vern shoveled in the last spoonful of chocolate pudding. He dropped the spoon to his tray and stood at the same time. "Practice after school?" he asked me.

I nodded.

"Later, Four-Twelve." Vern climbed from behind the bench and started walking toward the garbage can.

"Do you know what Mic calls you when you aren't around, VERNON? NERD BOY," Freemont said.

Vern didn't turn around; he just kept walking. "NERD BOY!" Freemont shouted at the top of his lungs. The tables to either side of the garbage can quieted, and everyone turned to look at Freemont. Everyone except Vern. He emptied his trash into the garbage can, stacked his tray, turned, waved, and walked away.

"Nerd Boy! Nerd Boy! Nerd Boy!" Freemont chanted. Two tables joined in. I jumped up and grabbed Freemont by the arm. "Cut it out."

"Or what? You'll *sock* me?"

My face was red. I felt like someone had already pounded me.

"Shut up!" I growled between my teeth. "Just leave him alone. Vern's not so bad. In fact, he's a good baseball player. Why don't you come and practice with us after school. Tryouts are next Saturday."

"You're kidding, right?"

"About what?"

"Trying out for the Pony League."

"Of course not. Why would I kid about that?"

"Little League is for kids. The Pony League is for wimps and nerds. Which one are you?"

"Shut up, Freemont."

Freemont unfolded his long legs and jumped up beside me, spilling a carton of milk in the process. We stood toe to toe.

"You think you can make me?" he breathed down on me.

Freemont is two inches taller than I am. He's tough, but I could take him if I had to.

"Fight! Fight!" someone shouted.

The tables around us quieted down. I could feel everyone watching us.

I clenched and unclenched my fists. I could hear the milk dripping from the table to the floor.

Stolks hopped up from the lunch table.

"Come on, guys."

I could feel Freemont's hot breath on the bridge of my nose.

"Anybody wanna share a Twinkie with me?" Stolks asked.

I gritted my teeth so hard they hurt. But I wasn't backing away.

"How about a Mounds bar?"

"Shut up, Stolks!" Freemont and I said in unison.

It was two, maybe three seconds before we broke out laughing. We left our trays on the table and ran for the door.

"Hey, wait for me," Stolks said, trying to gather the rest of his lunch.

Freemont and I turned from the door just in time to see the lunchroom monitor stop Stolks and make him clean up the table where we left our lunch and wipe up the milk from the floor.

Seeing Stolks on his hands and knees on the floor sent waves of laughter over the two of us. Freemont slapped me on my back and I slapped his. We started laughing and didn't stop until we had reached my locker.

After school we went our separate ways. I watched for Vern and his strange speed walking. I didn't see him. All the way home I expected him to pop up at my side. He didn't.

Chapter 24

"I knew you could do it" was all Mom said when I told her about my math test. I know she meant it as a compliment, but it made me feel like I hadn't tried before.

Stephanie hugged me and jumped up and down.

"Let's celebrate," Mom signed to Stephanie. They decided we would go bowling. Nobody asked me what I wanted to do.

I thought I would die every time Stephanie got up to bowl.

Mom led Stephanie to the foul line and pointed her in the right direction. Stephanie didn't bother putting her fingers in the holes. With both hands, she rolled the bowling ball from between her legs. The ball slowly started off down the alley. Stephanie shrieked as soon as the ball left her hands. She pulled at the fuzzy ends of her hair.

At first I didn't think the ball was going to make it down the alley. It seemed to come to a stop right in the middle of the lane. But it started moving again, creeping straight down the center. Right before it hit the head pin, it took a right turn. It barely hit the ten pin before it fell into the gutter. The ten pin toppled over in slow motion, falling toward the center of the pins. Slowly—one by one—pins fell in a wild, crazy pattern. When the pins stopped falling, only five were left standing.

Stephanie staggered back to the sitting area. She must have been counting steps, because she didn't trip on the step down from the approach way.

Mom showed her on a little model of ten miniature bowling pins which pins she had knocked over. Stephanie jumped up and down. It was the first time in four frames she had knocked down more than one pin. She had doubled her score. She had passed Ricky on the score sheet. If she was lucky, in the fifth frame she could rocket into double digits.

Ricky bowled the first three frames and lost interest. He sat behind the row of seats and played with Peanuts. I wish I could have been so lucky. Whenever Stephanie bowled, everyone in the building stopped and stared. I knew they were looking at the rest of us, trying to figure out what was wrong with us. When it was my turn, I threw the ball quickly and sat down again. I didn't look around a lot. Maybe if I didn't see anyone, they wouldn't see me, either.

I could have bowled a 170—that's my high game—but I was lucky I got the 126 that I did. I didn't care. I just wanted to get out of there.

After bowling, Mom decided we should go out for pizza. Thank God I talked her into carryout. Who knew whom we might run into at Tony's on a Friday night? We picked up two large pizzas and headed home.

Everything was going great. Mom was happy that we were doing something as a family. I think she's seen too many reruns of *Little House on the Prairie*. It was the perfect time to ask about the baseball glove.

"Dad . . . Mom . . . ," I said as I reached for another slice of pizza. "Vern has this nice glove. A Rawlings. A great glove." I took a bite of pizza. "It made me think . . . it would be nice if I could . . . See, I really do need . . . a new glove."

I looked carefully from Mom to Dad to see if they were listening.

"Ricky, please use your napkin," Mom said as she cut another slice of pizza. "You already have a glove, don't you?" she asked.

"Yeah, but the leather's cracked and the padding's gone," I said, pulling it out from under the chair.

"How much would a new glove cost?" Mom asked.

"Fifty . . . sixty dollars if we find a good deal," I hedged. I knew a new glove could run as high as $120.

"Sixty dollars?! For a baseball glove? Do you know what I could buy with sixty dollars?" Mom replied.

"Looks to me as if you have it well broken in," Dad said.

"Dad, it's four years old, and . . ." I looked at the glove as if it would magically persuade them. "Let's say I got a line drive up the middle and I caught it with this old glove. It would really burn." I shook my hand to emphasize the imagined pain.

"Maybe if you didn't play so rough," Mom said as she served Ricky another piece of pizza, "maybe you could get by."

"Get by!" I repeated. "Get by!" My face grew hot and the room dimmed. "I don't want to get by. I want to play in the Pony League. I want to be the best infielder the world has ever seen. And I can't do it with this old thing." I threw the glove on the floor.

"Now listen, Michael," Dad said, adjusting his glasses and sitting up straight. "Let's not get emotional. We'll take a look at this issue rationally."

Rationally, I thought. *That always means he's right and I'm not.*

"Go ahead and practice and try out for this team. They're interested in you, not your equipment."

"But, Dad, a better glove would help me play—"

"To put it simply, Michael," he said leaning forward on his arm, "I don't think the benefits outweigh the expense."

"But—" I panicked. I didn't know what to come back with. He wasn't going to budge; I looked around the room for something to help with my argument.

"We can afford a bowling pin model. We can afford special books and games, but we can't afford a baseball glove for me," I said.

Mom stiffened. "Don't try that," she growled. "Those items are pertinent to your sister's development. It's not—"

"It's not fair!" I finished for her. It was the first time since I skinned my leg wiping out on my bike that I felt like crying. Well, I wasn't going to cry. I wasn't.

"How can you talk about fair." Mom glared at me. "Look at your sister."

I looked across the table at Stephanie. She shoved a piece of pizza in her mouth and took another bite. A long string of mozzarella flopped out on her chin. She slurped it into her mouth and smacked loudly.

"She has been deprived—robbed of two major senses," Mom continued. "A bowling model, a few books, and special games are small compensation. Not getting a baseball glove is nothing in comparison." She shook her head and looked at me like I was a mass murderer or something.

"I'm sorry," I started to say. I could feel the tears coming. I jammed my fingernails into my palm to make them stop. I was *not* going to cry. "I'm sorry I was born normal. I'm sorry I can hear. I'm sorry I can see." I jumped to my feet and bumped the table as I stood.

The movement startled Stephanie. She put her hands out to steady the table. When she was sure that it was secure, her eyes flitted back in her head and she started gulp-laughing. She put her hand on Ricky's face, then on Mom's. Mom gently removed it. Ricky protested and moved away.

"R-R-R-R-EEEEE," she hooted as she started to tickle him.

I rushed around the table and scooped him up. "Come on, Ricky," I said as I rushed to my room. "If no one else is going to protect you from her, I'll have to."

I slammed the door. Hot tears stung my face. I stamped my foot; I'd promised myself I wasn't going to cry. I wiped the tears away with the back of my hand.

"Why are you crying?" Ricky asked, giving me a little hug.

I couldn't answer.

"It's OK, Michael. Let's play a game," Ricky suggested.

I was about to say no when I heard the voices in the other room.

"I don't see why we can't look into it," Dad was saying.

"That's blackmail," Mom shouted. "Emotional black-mail! He is trying to make us feel guilty just so he can get his way! I won't have it! I won't have it!"

"We can play Go Fish," Ricky said.

"Shh." I motioned to Ricky and put my ear to the door.

"Maggie, maybe we were too harsh. I don't know much about baseball. Maybe he *is* due for a new glove," Dad said.

"That's not the point," Mom said. "It's the way he went about it."

"We didn't give him many options. Let's just talk about it with him."

"We'll discuss it later. Ricky! Michael!" she bellowed. "Come finish your dinner NOW!"

I rubbed at my eyes and went back to the kitchen. I sat down at the table with a plop and shoved a piece of pizza into my face. It was cold.

I could see the veins standing out on Mom's neck. Her cheeks were still red. I had this strange feeling that she was on the verge of flipping out.

I decided not to ask about the glove again.

Chapter 25

I didn't see Vern all weekend. He called on Sunday to see if I wanted to go to the batting cages.

"Tell him I can't come to the phone right now," I said to Mom when Vern called.

He called back later, but I pretended to be asleep so I didn't have to deal with Mom or Vern.

I tried not to think about what happened in the lunch-room Friday. I tried not to think about what would happen on Monday. *Something* was going to happen. I knew that. Who knew what Freemont might come up with?

Even back in second grade, Freemont had been unpredictable. One day, for no reason at all, he just de-pantsed Jeff Ricker—right in the middle of afternoon recess. That's when I started calling him Wildman Freemont. Then last year while we were reviewing for our social studies test, Mrs. Wilson told Freemont to pick a girl next. He got that look in his eye and then he said, "Todd Baskin." Everyone burst out laughing, including Todd. Then all of a sudden, Todd's lip started to quiver, he started crying, and he ran from the room. That only made Freemont laugh harder. People still talk about the day Wildman Freemont called Todd Baskin a girl and made him cry.

The lunchroom buzzed. Everyone stared at our table. It was worse than I imagined. Freemont had covered his old science project board with a grocery bag. In large red letters that ran downhill it read NO NERDS ALLOWED. Below that he had drawn the international "no" sign crossed over a sock. It barely covered his project on acid rain.

Freemont was like a caged animal. He would take a bite, jump up, and look around the lunchroom. "Where is he?" he growled. Once he even stood on the bench and shouted out, "Come out! Come out wherever you are! Nerds in free!"

"I can't believe it," he grumbled. "For weeks the nerd sits here uninvited. The first time I *want* him to be here, he doesn't show up."

Vern wasn't in social studies or gym, either.

It was the same on Tuesday and Wednesday.

Thursday morning I saw him walking to school in a driving April rain.

"Should we give the new kid a ride?" Dad asked.

"No!" I shouted, as Dad slowed down.

Dad looked at me like I was out of my mind.

"Vern's on the cross-country team. This is part of his training. You know, walking and running in all types of weather."

"He certainly walks fast."

Nerd Boy's straight-legged speed walk propelled him down the street. Rain matted his bangs to his face. He didn't look over at us, but I knew he knew I was watching him. I got the funny feeling he even knew what Dad and I were talking about. Maybe he *is* an alien.

After school Freemont wanted to come over.

"Not today," I told him.

"Freaks on the loose at home again?"

"Big test in social studies tomorrow." Good thing Freemont doesn't have social studies with me or he'd know that the big test was last week.

When I walked in the door, I was glad Freemont wasn't with me. There were big labels on everything: CORDUROY. LEATHER. SILKY. PLEATED. VELVETEEN. Braille letters were punched out below. Mom must be working on another project with Stephanie.

"Corduroy?" I asked.

"Stephanie is learning texture words this week."

"Why did you print it out?" I asked.

"For Ricky," she answered. "He might as well learn the words at the same time."

Yes, of course! For Ricky! For Stephanie! I thought. *Never mind that I can never invite people to the house again.*

But this was better than the time we had the shoe in the refrigerator. I was only five then. Stephanie must have been about seven. The word of the week was *shoe*. Mom hid shoes everywhere Stephanie might find them. The refrigerator was definitely a good place to put one; Stephanie was always in the refrigerator. But before Stephanie found it, a kid I had invited home from kindergarten found it. I can't remember his name—he moved away years ago—but I do remember the look on his face.

"What is a shoe doing in the refrigerator?" he asked.

We looked around; there were shoes everywhere. There was a shoe attached to the wall like in the book *Wacky Wednesday*. There was a shoe in the fruit bowl on the kitchen table nestled in between the grapes and the bananas.

I didn't say anything. I was just a little kid. What could I say? A neighborhood shoe factory had recently exploded and this was the fallout?

I never invited him over again. And he never invited me to his house—like having me at his house would make it weird, too.

I'm glad Freemont hadn't come over today. Freemont

had seen his share of strange things in this house. I didn't know if I could take any more of his ribbing.

"I called Mrs. Freemont today," Mom said, as if she knew I was thinking about him.

"What for?"

"Did you forget? We leave for Boston tomorrow."

How could I forget? It was all anyone had talked about around the dinner table for two days. Dad called it a "fact-finding mission." Mom acted like she would be facing a firing squad. Stephanie was so excited you would have thought she was going to Disney World or something. "B-O-S-T-O-N M-A-S-S-A-C-H-U-S-E-T-T-S capital," she often signed during dinner.

"I thought you had worked out all the arrangements with David," Mom said.

"It must have slipped my mind. Where's Ricky staying?"

"The Bakers'. It's OK if you stay with the Freemonts, isn't it? Mrs. Freemont says she hasn't seen you in ages."

Had it been so long? I tried to remember the last time I had been to Freemont's house, but I couldn't. Last summer I had practically lived there.

Stephanie came into the room. She stopped, crossed her arms in front of her, and scowled. I realized she had copied my posture and facial expression exactly. How did she do that?

She gulp-laughed and then reached for me. I pulled away from her.

"Is it OK?" Mom asked.

"What?"

"That you're staying at Freemont's."

"Yeah, sure."

It felt funny that she had to ask. The whole thing felt funny.

Mom gets all freaky before she leaves on a trip. For some

reason she wants the house perfectly clean before we leave. She really went psycho this time because she was leaving Ricky and me behind.

All afternoon she had been doing laundry, cleaning anything that didn't move fast enough, and making lists.

She practically wrote my whole life history to give to Mrs. Freemont. Besides the seven or eight pages of facts about Ricky she wrote to give to Mrs. Baker, she had a shoe box full of medicine "just in case Ricky gets sick."

Thunder rumbled in the distance. Ricky ran into the kitchen and tugged on Stephanie's sleeve.

"T-H-U-N-D-E-R," he spelled in her hand.

Stephanie shrieked. Her eyes rolled back in her head. Her big smile made her look like a jack-o'-lantern. She grabbed Ricky's hand and started off toward the front window.

Some kids are afraid of thunder and lightning. Not Ricky. I wasn't, either. Stephanie made thunderstorms seem wonderful and magical. When I was Ricky's age and Stephanie was about seven, we'd camp out in front of the window on stormy nights. When lightning flashed, I would pat Stephanie's knee and we would put our hands on the window. When the thunder rumbled, even when it was soft and far away, you could feel it through the pane of glass. When the thunder was close, it would shake our insides.

I remembered how cool and wet the glass felt to my hand. When the wind was in the right direction, you could feel the rain pecking against the window. It was like being part of the storm.

Lightning flashed bright and close. Ricky patted Stephanie's knee. Stephanie shrieked and pulled on the fuzzy ends of her hair with her free hand, throwing her head back. Within seconds, thunder rumbled through the house.

Even though I didn't have my hand on the window, I could feel it. The rumbling moved through my feet up my legs to shake the middle of my stomach.

I couldn't remember the last time Stephanie and I had sat at the window feeling the thunder through the palms of our hands. It felt like so long ago.

Chapter 26

Dad offered to take me to Freemont's house, but I said I would rather walk. Mom shooed me out the door before they left. I don't think she trusted me to stay in the house by myself. Maybe she thought I'd forget to lock the door or leave the water running.

Inside, the house was clean and every last towel was folded, but Mom hadn't had a chance to clean the front picture window again. From the street you could see the handprints and smudges from the night before.

Freemont and I live at opposite ends of the Fossie Wiley Grade School boundaries. When we were little, we weren't allowed to ride our bikes the twelve blocks that separated us. For the first few years at Fossie Wiley, we were playground friends. By fourth grade, we were riding back and forth between our houses nearly every day. We found a shortcut through vacant lots that shaved the ride time down to eight and a half minutes if we rode at top speed and didn't stop at stop signs.

It had been a long time since I had ridden my bike to Freemont's house. I didn't take any shortcuts today.

Houses at Freemont's end of town were older, smaller, and closer together. The trees were bigger in this neighborhood. On this early April day, the trees were just beginning to leaf out.

I hadn't been in Freemont's room for a very long time. He had ripped down his baseball posters. In some places, the corners were still taped to the wall, but the rest of the poster had been torn away. In their place hung a bunch of dirt bike posters. The stereo was cranked up so loud, Stephanie could have felt every note.

I flopped facedown on the bed and hung my head over the edge. I lifted up the end of the bedspread to see what I would find. This was a game I played when I was in grade school. Our house isn't always clean, but Mom insists the floor be picked up so Stephanie won't trip over anything. Most of the time I just shove things under the bed or into the closet.

I thought the pile of things under my bed was bad, but Freemont's was worse. Once I'd found a petrified peanut butter and jelly sandwich. It was rock hard. Even the green-blue mold that had grown on it had passed the soft and furry stage and was hard as a rock.

I was surprised to see three egg cartons. I peeked inside the first one. Yes. It was full of eggs. I lifted the corners of the other two. They were full, too. Hopefully, they hadn't been there as long as the petrified peanut butter sandwich.

"Getting a jump on breakfast?" I asked.

"Eggs aren't just for breakfast." Freemont gave me a weird smile.

I checked out what was under the foot of the bed: a pile of clothes, a stack of magazines, wadded-up paper, at least a dozen gum wrappers, and three packages of toilet paper.

Later that night, Freemont pulled the eggs and TP out from under the bed. We put on our jackets and prepared to sneak out of the house. It wasn't the first time. Sneaking out of Freemont's house was easy. His father works the night shift so he is never home, and his mother has trouble sleeping so she leaves the TV on all night. She watches old movies, the black-and-white kind, with really disgusting music. She keeps the volume cranked way up. No wonder she has a hard time sleeping. At least she says she has a hard time sleeping. Whenever Freemont and I peek in her room, she's zonked. She sleeps propped up in bed with her head all the way back. She always has her mouth open and makes weird wheezing noises.

We waited until a loud commercial came on, then Freemont opened his bedroom window. I crawled out and dropped to the grass below. Freemont lowered the bag of eggs and toilet paper into my waiting hands, then slithered out the window.

A knot formed in my stomach as soon as we started out. It was after eleven and past curfew. According to the newspaper, the police were cracking down on curfew violators.

We stuck to the side streets, hugging the edges of houses and cutting through yards. I had been so worried about getting caught, I hadn't even thought about the target. Besides, Freemont seemed to know where he was going. I just followed.

I was so busy looking over my shoulder, I didn't realize where I was until we came up alongside the Pepto-Bismol house. We peeked out from behind a big prickly evergreen bush. It was obvious what our night's target would be—the house at the end of the cul-de-sac. Chortle's house. Mr. Chortle's Mustang convertible was parked in the driveway.

Freemont pulled a can of shaving cream from his pocket. NERD GO HOME he wrote on the grass of the front yard.

I was the lookout. I flattened myself against the corner of the house and nervously scanned the street.

"Come on," Freemont called to me.

Slowly, I peeled myself away from the house.

I had TP'ed houses before. I was good at tossing toilet paper in trees. As I started to throw a roll of toilet paper, I heard a screen door shut. The slam was followed immediately by the *yip-yip-yip* of Mr. Petrowski's bull terrier, Tiny. It was the yappiest dog on the block.

Tiny ran to the edge of his yard and stopped as if he knew exactly where his yard stopped and the Chortles' yard began. From there he yapped at us, each bark pulling his front paws off the ground.

Predictably, the screen door squeaked open again. I could imagine the webbed fingers of Mr. Petrowski holding open the door. "T-I-I-I-I-I-I-I-NNNNNNNYY!" Mr. Petrowski rasped in his cigarette-rough voice. I saw the glow of his cigarette in the night. Tiny didn't move toward him at all. He continued to bark and yap. "T-I-I-I-I-I-I-I-NNNNNNNYY! Come on, you silly nut," Mr. Petrowski called again. I lunged toward Tiny. He whimpered and ran home.

"Where's the Nerd's window?" Freemont asked as if he hadn't heard Tiny or Mr. P. There was only one thing on his mind. I don't think getting caught ever occurred to him. "On the side? In the back? Where is it?"

"It's over here." I pointed.

What if I was wrong? What if he accidentally hit Angela's window? She would sound the alarm in a minute, and I would be arrested for sure. I could hear Jessica now. "Our house never got egged in Ohio. I hate this crappy little town. It's filled with geeks, geeks, GEEKS!"

I looked behind me and expected to see Freemont.

"Freemont?" I called softly.

I looked down the street. It felt spooky. I wouldn't have been surprised to have seen Houdini's ghost. I heard *crunch! splat! crack! splat!*

"Freemont!" I almost said out loud but somehow managed a whisper. "Freemont, what are you doing? Not the car! Not the car! It can ruin the paint."

The porch light next door came on, and we ducked behind the small shrub to the right of the driveway.

Sam, the big three-legged golden retriever, bounded toward us. He barked once gruffly when he heard us in the bushes. Unlike Tiny, who barked constantly at anyone and anything, Sam only barked at people he didn't know. His bark would send people to the windows.

"Sh-h-h-h! Sam, it's me," I said. Then the tail wagged. I was home free. "Let's get out of here," I told Freemont.

"I still have more eggs."

"Leave them."

All the way home, I wondered if the cops could get fingerprints off egg cartons.

Chapter 27

"I have to get a drink," I told Freemont as soon as we crawled through his bedroom window. I slipped out his door and passed his mom's room. I peeked in. She was in the same position—sitting straight up with her head back and her mouth open. I tiptoed down the hall to the kitchen and picked up the phone. I pecked out Chortle's phone number, surprised that I knew it by heart.

"Hello?" a sleepy voice asked.

"Errr! Ahem." I cleared my throat trying to drop my voice two octaves. "Better wash your car." I hung up. The sooner Mr. Chortle could wash the eggs off, the less damage it would do.

I didn't sleep very well that night. When I did, I had strange dreams. Once I dreamed Angela and Jessica caught me. Angela was shouting, "Call the police!" But she couldn't call the police because Jessica was on the phone. When Jessica turned around, she was wearing a police cap and badge. "You're under arrest, geek," she said as she snapped handcuffs on me. "Geek! Geek! Geek!" she screamed at me over and over again as she slammed the door to my jail cell.

Another time I was in a court of law. A talking Tiny was on the witness stand. His voice was as high and yappy as his bark. "He did it," Tiny yapped, pointing at me.

"Could you please tell the court who egged Chortle's

car," the judge asked Sam next. Sam trotted from the witness stand right to me and lifted his leg on me. I woke up. I was wet. I smelled my shirt to make sure it wasn't dog pee. It was just sweat.

I tossed and turned the rest of the night. The next morning I woke exhausted. Freemont was in the kitchen hunched over a dirt bike magazine eating a bowl of cereal.

"Want some?"

I shook my head. Tryouts were at eleven and I knew I should eat something, but I wasn't hungry.

"My dad's going to get me a Model TX300 for my birthday. Ask your parents for one. We could go riding together," Freemont said.

My parents wouldn't buy me a new baseball glove. How could I talk them into buying me a dirt bike? I didn't want a dirt bike anyway. I didn't say anything to Freemont.

I went to Freemont's room and got dressed.

"You aren't really going to try out for the stupid Pony League, are you?" Freemont asked when he came into the room.

"Yes, I am."

"Maybe it's something in the water in your neighborhood."

"What's that supposed to mean?"

"If you don't know, I guess you are too far gone."

I looked around Freemont's room. It looked even more different in the bright sunlight. Who was this guy? When had he changed? Had I changed?

It wasn't about Nerd Boy and yet it was. I packed up all my things and threw the duffel bag over my shoulder.

"It doesn't look like you are planning on coming back," Freemont said as I walked out the door.

"I'm not."

"Good" was all he said. He slammed the door behind me.

I tried to remember the shortcuts that Freemont had made the night before, but I couldn't. I had to stick to the streets.

I wondered, as I walked, if Mrs. Freemont would notice I was missing. Luckily, I hadn't given her the list of emergency phone numbers Mom had made out for her.

By the time I turned onto Bixby Court, my bag was cutting into my shoulder. Our house looked quiet. As I walked by, the early morning sun spotlighted the handprints on the front window, making them stand out even more. Mom would die when she saw them, but they looked good to me just then.

Mr. Petrowski was hobbling out to the end of his driveway to get the morning paper. He was still in his bathrobe but had a cigarette in his mouth. Tiny trotted close at his heels. And even though Mr. Petrowski said no in his low, gravelly voice, Tiny yipped at me like I was an ax murderer or something.

I ignored Tiny and walked past the Pepto house and Mrs. Marston's. Sam was inside looking out the front window. He stood and wagged his tail when he saw me.

Mr. Chortle was out in front of his house waxing the car.

I glanced at the lawn. The morning dew had made the shaving cream melt into the grass. The budding trees had a nice draping of toilet paper blowing in the breeze.

I picked up a towel and started buffing.

"Hi! Mic." He smiled. "You don't have to help."

"I'm a little nervous about the tryouts today. This will get my mind off it."

I helped Mr. Chortle for about half an hour before Vern poked his head out the door and said, "Mic! Dad! Breakfast is ready." He acted as if I was supposed to be there all along.

The smell of warm cinnamon almost knocked me over as soon as I came through the front door.

"Good morning, Mic," Mrs. Chortle chirped. "We were just going to have breakfast. Won't you join us? Angela, set another spot."

"Thanks," I said, setting my duffel bag inside the kitchen door.

"Are you taking all that to the tryouts?" Mrs. Chortle asked.

"No. Well, see . . . I . . ." I blushed. I couldn't get the words to come out straight.

The rest of the family had started eating. Mrs. Chortle walked over to me, put her hand on my shoulder, and looked me straight in the eye.

"Is everything OK, Mic?" she asked softly, so the others wouldn't hear.

"Yes. Kind of . . . ," I stammered. I couldn't look her in the eye. "No. Not really."

She pulled me into the hallway and waited for me to collect my thoughts so I could finish.

"You see I was supposed to spend the weekend with Freemont. He's this guy. My parents are away visiting a school for my sister in Boston. But, well—things just didn't work out."

"Hmmm." Mrs. Chortle nodded. "I see."

"I was wondering—I mean if it's OK with you and Mr. Chortle . . . Could I stay here? It would just be tonight and tomorrow night. We could call my parents and let them know."

"Of course, Mic."

I wondered if it was OK with Vern.

No one said anything about the egging or the Nerd Boy sign on the lawn. I wondered if they knew.

"Ready, Daddy?" Jessica smiled. I think it was the first time I had seen her smile.

Angela pulled on my sleeve. "Jessica's all excited," she whispered in my ear, "because a bunch of boys TP'ed our house last night. She thinks she's popular."

"Ready," Mr. Chortle said, handing over the keys.

"I've driven the Mustang before," Jessica told me as she backed out. "But this is the first time with the top down."

"Where were you all week?" I asked Vern as we backed out of the driveway. It was the first time I had spoken to him since that day in the lunchroom over a week ago.

"I changed my schedule," he said. I couldn't tell if he was upset. "I tried to call you a couple of times."

"I've been busy."

There were about forty guys trying out for fifteen spots on the team. We stretched and went through drills. I wished I had a new glove for tryouts, but my old glove would have to do.

It didn't seem to matter. I did great at the second-base position. I fielded every ball hit my way except one. I doubt if Ozzie Smith could have gotten that one. I kept batting the way Mr. Chortle had taught me. I didn't have the fastest time running to first base, but it was respectable.

I wished they would have told us right then if we made the team, but the coach said he would call everyone on Sunday. I made sure he knew I was staying at Chortle's house for the weekend.

Mr. Chortle and Jessica watched the tryouts from the stands. He didn't say anything to us when we were finished, just patted us on our backs and smiled. I think that was a good sign. He treated us to pizza at Tony's. Jessica sat across from me. I had a hard time keeping my eyes off her. Her hair's so beautiful. Even though I was starved, I only ate a few pieces. I found it hard to eat when she was looking at me.

Vern hadn't said much of anything to me all day. But then that wasn't unusual.

Chapter 28

"You went to Tony's without *me?*" Angela screamed when we got home. She threw her sweatshirt at us and stomped up the stairs.

Nobody said anything.

Jessica rolled her eyes and followed her upstairs.

I called my parents. Mom didn't seem mad that I was at the Chortles'. "Be polite" was all she said.

Mrs. Chortle popped a huge bowl of popcorn while I was on the phone. I joined Vern and his parents in the family room. They have a big-screen TV with Surround Sound speakers. We started to watch the first of two videos we had picked up on the way home from Tony's.

About halfway into the first movie, it started raining. The first clap of thunder brought Angela out of hiding. She rocketed down the stairs and leaped into her father's lap.

She buried her head in her father's shirt. "I hate thunder," she said.

"I love thunder," I said. "Our whole family does."

"You mean *your* sister isn't afraid of storms?" Vern asked.

"Stephanie? Stephanie isn't afraid of anything," I said.

"How about your little brother?" Angela asked. "I bet he's afraid of storms."

"Nope! He loves 'em. In fact, I bet right now he's at the

Bakers' house with his hand on the window so he can feel the thunder."

"Feel the thunder?" she asked, looking up from her father's chest long enough to give me a strange look.

A clap of thunder sent her burrowing against his plaid shirt again.

"You wouldn't be afraid either, Angela, if you felt it. It's pretty cool."

I told Vern and his parents about our nights at the front window.

Mrs. Chortle walked to the sliding-glass door and placed her hand on the glass just in time to feel a sharp clap followed by rolling thunder.

"Wow!" was all she said.

Angela ran to her mother's side and felt the next rumblings.

"Cool! Vern, come feel this!" Angela shrieked.

Vern went over to the window. Mr. Chortle followed. Every rumble sent a wave of giggles through Angela. Jessica came downstairs and had to feel the thunder for herself.

"It sends shivers down my spine," she said. The way she said it sent shivers down *my* spine. Jessica put her cheek against the cool pane of the sliding-glass door and pressed her whole body against the door. The wind shifted and sent raindrops pecking against the glass just as a clap of thunder shook the whole house. "Totally awesome," Jessica breathed out.

"Stop hogging the glass," Angela said, nudging Jessica aside. "Let me feel it." Angela pressed her cheek against the glass first and then her whole body. "I can feel the wind," she said, not to be outdone by her sister.

If anyone had walked into the room right then, they'd have thought we were all a bunch of wackos. Every inch of glass was covered. Angela and Jessica both had their cheeks, arms, and full bodies pressed against the glass.

Mr. and Mrs. Chortle and I were content to have just our hands against the glass till Vern shucked off his shoes, peeled off his Shark Attack socks, and put his feet on the sliding-glass door. "I've got to get some socks with lightning bolts on them," he said, his Cheshire cat smile making his eyes disappear into tiny squinty half-moons behind his huge glasses. Even I'd never tried feeling the thunder through my feet. Jessica, Angela, and I ripped off our shoes and socks and felt the thunder reverberating through the soles of our feet until the storm rumbled way off into the distance and we could barely feel it on the sliding-glass doors.

"I'll never think of thunderstorms the same way," Jessica said as she gathered up her socks and shoes.

"No fair!" Angela wailed. "I didn't get to feel the really big thunder at the beginning of the storm."

"There'll be other storms," Mrs. Chortle said.

"I never thought my Angela would ever look forward to a thunderstorm," Mr. Chortle said, giving her a hug.

We'd missed most of the second half of the movie. While Mr. Chortle rewound the video, Mrs. Chortle refilled our drinks.

"So Stephanie may be going to school in Boston this fall?"

"Yes. That's why my parents took her to visit the school."

"Your mother must be a wreck. Boston is so far away. I'm already a wreck thinking about Jessica going away to college, and that's two years away."

"Mother, PUH-LEEZE," Jessica said. She rolled her eyes, jumped up, and stalked from the room as if she had just received the biggest insult of her life.

"I don't think Mom thought Stephanie would ever go away to school." I know I never had.

"How is Stephanie taking this? Is she scared about being so far away from home?"

Stephanie scared? The idea made me smile.

"Not Stephanie," I said, shaking my head. "She has a way of turning the tiniest thing into a big adventure. This is a mega-adventure for her."

"I think this is about where we left off," Mr. Chortle said, clicking "play" on the remote.

It was well after midnight when we got through the second movie. Mrs. Chortle had fallen asleep on the couch. Vern and I mouthed "good night" to Mr. Chortle and tip-toed upstairs.

Even though I hadn't gotten much sleep the night before, I couldn't fall asleep. Lying there in the darkness, I could see. I could hear. I put my fingers in my ears. No matter how hard I tried to plug my ears, I could still hear my own breathing and Vern's snoring. It was dark, but from the dim glow of the streetlight, I could still see shapes.

Somewhere, a thousand miles away, Stephanie was lying in a strange bed. Did the room feel different to her? Or was her dark, silent world the same no matter where she was? I could almost see her in my mind lying there in a strange bed, in a strange room, in a strange city. She'd have that big smile on her face. She would be able to feel the difference— and she would love it. What I had told Mrs. Chortle was true. Stephanie wasn't afraid of anything. To her, the world was a giant toy, and she couldn't wait to get her hands on it and make it her own.

I lay awake half the night. So many thoughts galloped through my head: tryouts, Stephanie in Boston, the thunder-storm, egging Vern's house, and that awful day in the lunch-room—the day Freemont blurted out that I called Vern "Nerd Boy."

Vern had never said anything about it. Maybe he hadn't heard. Maybe it hadn't mattered. I shut my eyes and could hear Freemont chanting, "Nerd Boy! Nerd Boy!" Vern had heard. He *had* to have heard. How could it *not* matter?

The next morning I slept in. Even the smell of Mrs. Chortle's baking didn't coax me out of bed. It was almost noon before I stumbled down the stairs.

The recent rain had caused an explosion of green. The trees were leafing out. The sliding glass door was full of handprints and smudges. I felt at home.

Mr. Chortle took us to the batting cages again. I was thankful to be doing something active. His bursts of Italian song didn't bother me as much as they had on our first visit.

The phone call came right after dinner. We both made the team! We all piled into the car and went down to the Tastee-Freez to celebrate.

I called Mom after we got back. "We made the team," I told her. "Both of us."

"Congratulations," she said. "Tell Vern I'm happy for him, too." But I didn't think she sounded very excited. She said they would be back when I got home from school tomorrow.

Mrs. Chortle made us go to bed early since it was a school night.

"And no staying awake talking," she warned us.

Was she joking or what?

"Vern," I asked right after he turned out the lights.

"Yeah?"

"Thanks for all your help. I don't know if I would have made the team if your dad hadn't helped me."

"Sure you would have."

Vern didn't talk much. It made it hard for me to say something about what had happened in the lunchroom last week.

"Vern?" I asked. "About what Freemont said in the lunchroom last week . . ."

There was only silence from his side of the room. I didn't hear snoring so I figured he was still awake.

"Freemont wasn't lying. I used to call you Nerd Boy."

I heard Vern breathe in.

"Vern?" I couldn't see his face, but I figured it was expressionless as always.

"I've been called worse."

"Doesn't it bother you?"

I could almost hear him shrugging.

I hadn't called him Nerd Boy in a couple of weeks, but I still felt bad that I had. "I'm sorry."

"I didn't ask if it was OK to call you Four-Twelve."

"At least you did it to my face, not behind my back."

I hated to admit it, but I kind of liked being called Four-Twelve.

It was quiet on the other side of the room. I could see his big nose silhouetted in the darkness.

"Vern? I was wondering . . . Would it be OK . . . I mean I would really like . . . Would you show me your sock collection?"

I could almost see him smile before he clicked on the light.

Chapter 29

Stephanie got her acceptance letter to the school in Boston the afternoon of our first game. She was so excited, she glowed. She read the letter over and over again. If she knew Mom was in her room crying, it didn't bother her. She clunked down the stairs to the basement looking for a suitcase to start packing, even though she wasn't leaving until August.

I went to the game early with the Chortles. Stephanie must have torn herself away from packing. I saw Mom, Dad, Stephanie, Ricky, and Peanuts file into the stands shortly after the first pitch.

Vern was starting pitcher. He went into his windup for the second pitch. I pulled at the sleeve of my uniform. It was brand-new and still stiff. Coach gave me a weird look when I requested the number forty-two. It was as close to Four-Twelve as I could get.

I took my stance—legs spread wide, crouching down a bit, hands resting lightly on my knees. I glanced down at my glove. A brand-new Rawlings. I inhaled. The smell of new leather filled my nostrils.

When Mom and Dad arrived home from Boston, they had the glove with them with a big red bow tied around the webbing and a tag that read CONGRATULATIONS, MICHAEL!

"We thought the Pony League's new second baseman could use this," Mom said.

Stephanie sniffed the air and picked up the glove. She inhaled deeply. She felt the glove all over until she found where her hand went in. She slipped it on her hand and smacked it with her right.

"Ba-ball!" she hooted as she tried to say *baseball.*

Mom and Dad laughed.

Stephanie beamed.

I could see her smile as I glanced briefly at the stands. I pulled my hat down till it was almost over my eyes. I glared at the batter. The pitch. The swing. The batter popped up to short center field. Matthews easily caught it.

"One down and two to go," I called to Vern. He turned and looked at me. No hint of a smile on his lips. He pulled on his socks. I wondered what he would do when the elastic was finally shot in his lucky Nolan Ryan socks.

Their second batter made it to base on a bunt, but we erased him when we turned a 5-4-3 double play.

I was batting sixth on the team. As I sat in the dugout waiting for my turn at bat, I wondered what life without Stephanie would be like.

Earlier that day, Mrs. Chortle asked me how I felt about Stephanie leaving. I told her I wasn't sure. Part of me was delirious! This was what I had always wanted. The other part of me felt guilty. "A little happy, a little sad, a little guilty," I told Mrs. Chortle.

"Why do you feel guilty?" Angela asked, popping up from behind the kitchen counter.

I shrugged. I didn't know how to put it into words. "I wanted Stephanie to go away so badly that I feel like I made it happen somehow," I finally said.

"That's how you feel. But do you really believe you made it happen?" Mrs. Chortle asked.

"No, I guess not," I replied.

She told me what I felt was normal. I didn't think anything about my life had ever been normal.

I didn't get to bat in the first inning. We got two hits but no runs.

I got a walk my first time at bat in the bottom of the second. I hung on and eventually scored a run.

In the third inning we knocked them down quickly. Three up and three down.

We scored another run in the bottom of the third.

The fourth inning was a long one. I thought we'd never get them out. They scored three runs. Finally, the center fielder popped one up right to me, and I caught the ball for the third out. As I jogged into the dugout, I thought about getting Stephanie a going-away gift.

Actually, Vern suggested it. He said even though his sisters were a real pain, he would probably miss them if they left.

"Especially Angela," he said. "Who would I have to make fun of anymore?"

I thought maybe I would buy Stephanie some modeling clay. She likes sculpting. But that didn't seem quite right.

Mom's worried that Stephanie will be afraid or confused about going away to school. But I know she's excited, not scared. "I will be with Deanie," she signed to me.

Bottom of the fourth, it was time to rally. We got some good chatter going in the dugout. Matthews stepped up to bat. He was our best hitter.

"Get a hit," I shouted to him.

I could see a large box by the concession stand. It made

me think about the spaceship Stephanie and I had made from a big cardboard washing machine box. I must have been about Ricky's age. We played in that thing for weeks. Mom said I understood Stephanie better than anyone else and I had been so proud.

Matthews popped up. Our hopes for a rally fizzled as they knocked us out of the inning: one, two, three.

By the time the last inning rolled around, we were down four to three. I had been on base three times in three at bats. I had two walks and a single. I had scored one run. We had to hold them here, then score two to win.

The first batter smacked one into short center field for a base hit. The second batter approached the plate. I knew he was good. It was a toss-up whether his strength was his speed or his hitting. He let the count go the full three and two before he caught one of Vern's sliders and hit a line drive up the middle. I was standing near second base. I scooped the ball off the turf, stepped on the bag, and rocketed the ball over to Jennings at first base. We nipped the runner just in time for the double play. I could hear Stephanie hooting in the stands.

One more out to go and we'd be up.

The batter popped up to our third baseman. He faded back to make the catch.

We had held them, but we were still down four to three. It was rally time.

Vern was up and I was on deck. Vern hit a blooper that dropped in the hole at short right center. Vern never looked at the ball but put his head down and ran for first base. He beat the throw in by only one step.

Vern represented the tying run. I represented the winning run. I had to get on base.

I stepped into the batter's box and stared at the pitcher.

The first pitch was high. It whizzed past me. I heard it zing into the catcher's mitt.

"Ball one!" the ump cried.

"Good eye. Good eye," the guys shouted from the bench.

My hands were sweating. I stepped out of the batter's box and rubbed some loose dirt on my bat. *Come on,* I thought. *Throw me a good pitch. I don't want to walk again.*

The second pitch zoomed past me. It was low.

"Ball two," the ump bellowed.

"Come on," I muttered as I squeezed the bat and gritted my teeth. "Throw me a good pitch!" If he threw a good pitch, I'd hit it into right field. I'd been watching their team closely all game. Their right fielder was the worst fielder on the team.

I thought the third pitch was low and outside, but it must have caught the lower corner because the ump called, "Strike one!"

The count was two and one. I stepped out of the batter's box and pulled at my sleeve. My new uniform was still stiff.

I looked at the stands and saw my family sitting in the third row. All except Stephanie. She was standing with one arm stretched out toward me as if she could feel what I was doing from there. Mom was holding her other hand. She let out a squeal I could hear all the way at home plate.

"Get a hit," the team chanted.

I stepped back into the batter's box. The next pitch was a little higher than I liked but hittable. I smacked it down the first baseline and past their right fielder. The ball bounced into the corner. I put my head down and dug for first base.

The first-base coach motioned for me to go on to second. The right fielder must have bobbled the ball—the way I hoped—because the third-base coach signaled for me to come on to third and take home.

As I rounded third base, I could hear Stephanie. "MY-Y-Y-Y-Y-Y-Y." Her shrill nasal voice cut through the noise of the crowd.

I slid headfirst into home plate, easily beating the throw in. I hadn't seen Vern score before me, but he was there at the plate shouting and screaming. It was the first time I had ever seen him excited. He looked more normal somehow.

Stephanie was still jumping up and down in the stands.

"Could I keep that ball?" I asked the ump as my teammates slapped me on the back.

"Sure, kid," he said, tossing it to me.

I caught the ball and hung on to it tightly as my team hoisted me into the air.

Chapter 30

The summer went by too quickly. Stephanie left for school two weeks ago. Mom spent most of August running around packing up things. You would have thought she was preparing for a moon launch with all the lists and checklists she had.

Mom shipped most of Stephanie's stuff to her school in four big boxes a week before she left for Boston; so when Stephanie left, she only had to take a small carry-on bag with her. Mom flew out to Boston with Stephanie. Dad, Ricky, and I hugged Stephanie good-bye at the airport.

Before she left, Stephanie gave us a little day calendar.

"Tear off each day," she said. "Number at bottom is number of days to wait before I come home." Stephanie smiled. Her eyes flitted back in her head. "I have calendar, too," she added. "We count days together."

Driving back from the airport, things seemed quiet. I couldn't resist putting my hand on the window as we drove home. I wondered if Stephanie had a window seat on the plane and if she had her hand stretched flat on it, feeling the miles that were going to separate her from her family.

Ricky was sitting in the backseat holding the day calendar on his lap.

"Stephanie'll be home in ninety-eight days," I told him.

When we picked up Mom at the airport two days later,

she didn't say a word. Her eyes were red and puffy, like she had cried during the whole flight. She hugged each one of us hard. I expected her to tell us about Stephanie's dorm and roommate, but Mom didn't say anything in the car the entire trip home.

"Things will be different at your house," Mrs. Chortle had warned me. "Be extra nice to your mom for a few days."

After the long, quiet ride home, I expected the house to feel different—like there would be a huge Stephanie void I would feel as soon as I walked through the door—but the house seemed the same. Even the texture cards were hanging in every room in the house. Mom decided to leave them up. "For Ricky," she said.

School started last week. Mom went back to teaching third grade. I bet it feels funny to have twenty-one students instead of just one. Ricky started kindergarten this year. Peanuts stayed home in the closet.

"Kingergarten is fun," Ricky told us at the dinner table that night. "I like Ms. Robbins."

I started eighth grade—my last year of junior high before high school. It was the first time since second grade I didn't have any classes with Freemont. We don't even have the same lunch hour. I didn't see much of him all summer. I made lots of new friends on the baseball team. We lost only four games and came in second in the league. I know we'll get the championship next year.

It turns out that Vern has *three* interests: baseball, socks, and totally gross jokes. He started telling the team jokes during a rain delay one afternoon. He had us all rolling around in the dugout.

The Chortles' house became the team hangout after that. Between Mrs. Chortle's baking and Vern's jokes, we always had a good time. I don't think anyone thinks of Bixby Court as a weirdo street anymore.

Vern and I have three classes together this year: gym, social studies, and home ec. I have Mrs. Propst for pre-algebra. She's not so bad. She laughs a lot and jokes around with us. We took our first quiz last week. I got a B and she didn't ask for anyone to have their parents write how they felt about their kid's grade on the back of the quiz.

Julia Patterson likes Russell Maxwell this year. Every time she sees me, she shoves her nose in the air and walks the other way, like I might try to talk to her or something. Flaky.

There is one girl that I'm glad to see. Wendy Parry. She's new and fits right in between Parrish and Parson for locker assignments. That puts me one locker away from Godzilla Girl. I wish it were more like thirty. Wendy's not bad for a girl; in fact, she's kind of cute.

Wendy lives a block over. We walked home from school together this afternoon. She told me she'd forgotten her pre-algebra book, and I told her she could borrow mine if she wanted. When she showed up at my front door an hour later, I got all nervous and felt funny because I was worried that Stephanie would clomp down the hall and embarrass me. With a pang, I remembered Stephanie didn't live here anymore.

Wendy was staring at the texture cards. I watched her eyes move from PLEATED to VELVETEEN to CORDUROY. "Corduroy?" she asked.

"Oh, my mom's a teacher." I shrugged. "She's into teaching vocabulary. You should hear my little brother. I bet he has the best vocabulary in his kindergarten class."

"What's this?" Wendy asked, pointing to a braille letter from Stephanie lying on the top of the mail pile on the coffee table.

"It's from my sister, Stephanie. She's deaf and blind. She just went away to school in Boston."

"What's it say?" she asked.

"I don't know—I haven't had a chance to read it yet. Let's see."

I took the letter and ran my fingers over the first row of raised dots. "Saturday, September fifth," I read out loud to Wendy.

"You read braille?" Wendy asked, as if it were the most amazing feat.

I shrugged. "Sure, and I know sign language, too. Well, just a little. Stephanie uses fingerspelling more than signs now that she's lost her sight, and I've forgotten lots of the signs I used to know."

If Stephanie had been there, Mom would have wanted her to meet Wendy. Mom would have fingerspelled Wendy's name into Stephanie's hand, and Stephanie would have felt Wendy's soft brown hair, silky skin, and cute turned-up little nose. At least her hair looks soft and her skin looks silky. Stephanie would have gulp-laughed and teased me about having a girlfriend. The thought of feeling Wendy's silky brown hair made me blush.

"I've always wanted to learn sign language," she said. "Can you teach me something?"

"Sure," I said. "This is Wendy," I said, fingerspelling it to her at lightning speed.

"But how could your sister see that if she's blind?"

"Oh, I'd fingerspell it into her hand like this," I said as I took Wendy's hand in mine. My whole body tingled as I fingerspelled her name into her hand.

"That's *so* cool. You'll have to show me more," she said. "But first the letter. Read me the letter."

"Saturday, September fifth," I repeated. Wendy sat back

on the couch staring up at me like I was a miracle worker. I cleared my throat and continued.

Dear Family,

I like new school. Math harder than Mom teached but fun. Today roommate Melinda and I walked. It is fall. I feel big piles of leaves. Must be many trees.

Teacher say Boston old city. Paul Revere's house not far. I must go visit.

Tonight Deanie sat with me dinnertime. She likes it here. I do, too.

Roommate touch Michael's baseball. I remember he hit it far for home run and win game. Roommate say she want to meet my baseball star brother.

Love,

Stephanie

"She must like you a lot," Wendy said.

"We've been close, I guess." I shrugged.

"Sounds like she's lucky to have you for a brother," she said.

"Actually, I'm lucky to have Stephanie for a sister," I said. "But you can judge for yourself. She'll be home in eighty-four days," I said, surprised that I remembered the actual number from the day calendar.

Mom kept it in the kitchen by the telephone.

Mom said Stephanie kept her calendar on her bedside table.

I imagined her reaching for it as soon as she woke up every morning. Her hair would frizz wildly away from her face. She would tear off the top sheet and feel how many days were left until she came home. I could almost see her goofy smile and hear her gulp-laughing.

Some things never change.